P9-DNI-452

Praise for *World of Pies:*

"Like fine chocolates, these sequential stories about a girl named Roxanne growing up in Annette, Texas, have a smooth, sweet exterior that conceals a surprise inside."

—*Booklist*

"If you're feeling stressed, but can't afford that getaway weekend in the Caribbean—don't despair. Grab your lawn chair, find a patch of filtered sun, inhale deeply and enter Karen Stolz's *World of Pies.*"

—*BookPage*

"With each slice from *World of Pies,* we taste the sweet and sour events of Roxanne Milner's life as she grows from a precocious nine-year-old to a mature adult of 38. Readers are left with that pleasant feeling at the end of a satisfying meal—that a nice long nap will follow."

—*Library Journal*

"A literary treat that is itself rich, slightly nutty, and almost impossibly sweet."

—*Texas Monthly*

"Hilarious and heartbreaking."

—*Seventeen*

"Karen Stolz's *World of Pies* is a charming portrait of small-town family life. It will make you wish you grew up with Roxanne."

—Ann Hood, author of *Ruby* and
Somewhere Off the Coast of Maine

"[*World of Pies*] gives new meaning to the phrase 'Home, sweet home.'"

—*People*

"This novel is as American as apple pie—Texas style. Yahoo!"

—Rita Mae Brown, author of *Outfoxed* and *Loose Lips*

"Oh, the powerful and diverting pleasures of the small town! I was reminded of early McMurtry, except *World of Pies* features a girl with a village of her own. Young Roxanne, as she blunders across every rite and every passage between the Hi-Ho Café and Carl's Corsets in the beguiling hamlet of Annette, Texas, has me absolutely charmed. This is a big-hearted human story, a world of pies, with such creatures in it!"

—Ron Carlson, author of *Hotel Eden: Stories*

"Just right for slipping into carry-on luggage or a bag bound for the pool or beach."

—*Austin Chronicle*

"The recipes are well-written and work, something of a rarity in works of fiction."

—*Fort Worth Morning Star-Telegram*

"For guaranteed summer reading pleasure, try Karen Stolz's *World of Pies*."

—*Charlotte Observer*

World
of Pies

World

of Pies

A NOVEL

Karen Stolz

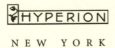

NEW YORK

Copyright © 2000 by Karen Stolz

All rights reserved. No part of this book may be used or reproduced in any manner whatsoever without the written permission of the Publisher. Printed in the United States of America. For information address Hyperion, 77 West 66th Street, New York, NY 10023-6298.

Library of Congress Cataloging-in-Publication Data

Stolz, Karen.
    World of pies : a novel / by Karen Stolz.—1st ed.
      p.   cm.
    ISBN 0-7868-6550-4
    1. Texas—Social life and customs Fiction. 2. City and town life—Texas Fiction. 3. Young women—Texas Fiction. 4. Family—Texas Fiction. I. Title.
PS3569.T6239W67 2000
813'.54—dc21   99-37294
              CIP

Paperback ISBN 0-7868-8462-2

Book design by Lisa Stokes

First Paperback Edition

10 9 8 7 6 5 4 3 2 1

For my mom and dad,
who gave me the gifts of
a small-town childhood and their
love of words,
and for my brave and true sisters,
Maggie and Katie,
and for my son Danny,
who is my heart and soul.

World of Pies

Acknowledgments

Thanks to my agent, Gail Hochman, and my editor, Leigh Haber, for loving my book and making it better. Thanks to my All-Girl Writing Group, Nancy Taylor Day, Ricki Ratliff, and Sandra Bybee, for their tender editing and abiding love. Thanks to John Taliaferro for being the first Roxanne fan. Thanks to Herman Wright for empowering me. Thanks to Tom Grimes for showing me the ropes. Thanks to the Iowa Writers Workshop for teaching me how to write a story. And thanks to all my dear friends, always.

World of Pies

THE SUMMER OF 1962, THE YEAR OF THE PIE FAIR, I WAS WILD FOR BASEBALL. I'D SLIP OUT JUST AS IT WAS COMing light, wearing cutoff denims and one of my dad's old T-shirts, washed and worn to transparency. My mother made me wear an undershirt beneath, as if there were something to hide. I ran to the ballpark flat-footed, scuffing my tennis shoes against the grainy sidewalk for traction. If I got there early enough, my cousin, Tommy, would pitch me a few balls to kill time before the boys showed up.

It was a Monday in early June. It was still cool at this hour; sometimes there was even a breeze. I tossed the baseball back and forth to myself as I walked. "Morning, Roxanne!" a neighbor or two would holler, Mrs. Fern letting out her cat, or Mr. Breebock picking up his newspaper from the sidewalk, or if he was lucky, his porch. I would pause in my ball tossing to wave. I knew everyone; like my daddy said, Annette, Texas, was a town small enough to know everybody, big enough to pretend we didn't when needed.

Since Tommy was an only child like me, we were more like siblings than cousins. When we were six, he had cut my favorite doll in half. I remembered him dangling her before my eyes, how I watched the sawdust sift out of her stomach. But now that we were twelve, we were friendlier. I was especially nice to him that summer, so he would help me with my pitching. This particular morning I was lucky. Tommy helped me for a good twenty minutes before the boys got there. When he grabbed my arms to show me how to hold the bat, he was a little rough; I liked that he treated me like the boys. He smelled like salty dirt, and his lank blond hair nearly hid his dark green eyes.

When I got home that morning my mother handed me a cool, soapy facecloth and a tall glass of orange juice clicking with ice cubes. "Rinse yourself off and help me with these pies," she told me.

She was already in full swing with her pie baking before eight. The dusting of flour on her eyelashes reminded me of snow on a Christmas tree. After I'd cleaned baseball dust from my face and all up and down my arms, she would apply a frilly apron to me. One minute I had a baseball bat in my hands, the next a rolling pin with bright red handles. My heart wasn't in it. Baking seemed trivial, a waste of my batting arm.

There was a lot of excitement in Annette, Texas, that summer. It was my father who came up with the idea of the pie fair. The Chamber of Commerce wanted to promote community spirit and drum up a little tourist business, too. The fair would be held the Fourth of July weekend. Everything would be pie-related: handmade aprons, tablecloths, pottery pie plates. Children would make pot holders and there would be a Miss Cherry Pie and a King Key Lime.

My father owned a lingerie store called Carl's Corsets. He took a lot of ribbing about his part in the fair. "Yessiree, Carl. Nothing an out-of-town visitor likes to do more after buying a hunk of pie than go browse through brassieres!"

In those days, I was extremely embarrassed about my father's line of work. Everyone around town joked about how he must know who was a D-cup and who wore the black merry widows that were occasionally displayed in the back of the store. But mostly my father hid out in his office adjacent to the store or perched in a neutral zone like handkerchiefs and gloves in the front; these he sold himself from time to time. He hired blue-haired ladies to assist his customers with their delicate purchases.

My mother met my father when she worked at the store one summer. She was the niece of one of the blue-haired ladies. She was considerably younger than my father, and he was so flustered to see soft, young hands folding the papery crinolines that he asked her out. My mother claims he married her so he wouldn't have to decide what to order for the store anymore. Before he married my mother, all his goods were white and stiff-looking. With my mother in his life, blush pink, blue enchantment, and lavender dusk slipped into the store, in satin peignoirs and lush petticoats. Business boomed. My father had never meant to be a lingerie salesman; the business had been left to him by an uncle. But my father accepted his fate, using his accounting skills to tally pajama sales instead of stocks and bonds.

His seat on the Chamber of Commerce was my father's real passion, next to my mom and me, and since the pie fair was his brainchild, he worked over the plans during his lunch hours and after dinner each night. He asked for my thoughts on promotion, and I knew when I had an idea he would listen. But mostly I just had ideas for pitching better, schemes for eluding my mom's pie-baking instructions.

When word got out about the pie fair, women all over Annette began perfecting their recipes. My father used to say if someone had flown a helicopter over Annette that summer they'd have seen a mist of flour rising from the town. There was a lot of discussion about the virtues of glass versus tin pie pans, cornstarch versus arrowroot for thickening pie juices. My mother was on a committee to determine the rules of the contest. All pies were to be made completely from scratch, they decided: no canned pie fillings or pudding mixes. And no collaboration. The flyer they printed read: "Your sister-in-law's crusts are divine but her fillings are watery, and your crusts are like sawdust but your fillings are a dream? Too bad, you do it all yourself." Of course, there was no way of knowing. No pie spies posted at kitchen windows, peering through gingham curtains.

My mother was determined to teach me how to make a piecrust. She wanted me to enter the junior homemaker division of the contest. I complained bitterly, but I fooled around some with the dough anyhow. In a tiny town like Annette there is nothing whatsoever to do in the summer, so the pie thing was something, anyway. My early efforts produced crusts with craters and little in the way of flavor.

"Roxanne, honey, you don't have to beat on that dough. You act like that rolling pin is a baseball bat!" my mother cried.

Then she demonstrated on a separate bowl of dough. The gold crumbs gathered to her fork magically, cleaving in seconds to a perfect round. She baked for hours every day the weeks before the fair. I knew she was very good at it, but pie baking was no spectator sport. My dad and I were baseball fans; we'd leave my mother to the world of pies.

"Were those apples from the Winemeyer orchard better than these?" my mother asked my father. He tested slice after slice of various pies for firmness and flavor.

"Exquisite, Christina. Juicy, and that crust just melts in my mouth. But . . . a mite too much lemon juice I think." He puckered his lips, making us laugh.

The same was going on in houses all around town. Delivery boys wheeled ten-pound sacks of sugar and flour to homes, comparing tips and arm muscles among themselves. The grocery stores ran specials and counterspecials. BROWN SUGAR A DIME! display windows beckoned.

My mother asked me to serve coffee when the contest rules committee met at our house about two weeks before the Fourth of July kickoff. I was edgy, bored, and hot, and I felt like a fool wearing an apron Mom had appliquéd with pie slices. The ladies were going on about tablecloth colors as I took an empty creamer to the kitchen for refilling, and the next thing I knew, something was going on, out in the living room. Evidently it had come out that the sweet potato pie Emma Reed intended to enter in the contest would be baked by Mary Willis, a black woman who did her cooking and ironing; it was Mrs. Willis's own recipe. Mrs. Reed had meant to slip it into the contest as her own.

I walked out to the living room with the pitcher filled with half-and-half.

"So what if the girl made it. Of course I'm going to enter it in the contest. It comes from *my kitchen!*" Mrs. Reed gulped some too-hot coffee, and I noticed her lipstick was smeared at the edges of her mouth.

"Christina, be reasonable," Josie Buford said. "No one but Emma's colored girl can make a sweet potato pie this good."

"There's no debating that the pie is delicious," my mother said, accepting the cool pitcher from me. "The point is, Emma didn't make this pie, Mary Willis did. The pie should be entered under Mary's name."

I missed what happened next because Tommy came knocking at the back door, wanting me to help him with some display tables he was building for the fair. My mother said I could go, and I immediately ripped off my apron and threw it in the kitchen sink. I wished Tommy hadn't seen me in that stupid checked sundress my mother made me wear for the committee ladies. How would he ever take me seriously as a baseball player?

"You'll get dirty," he warned me.

"I don't care," I assured him. Now that Tommy and I were walking on the sizzling street all I could think of was my half-slip twisting and clinging to the sweat on my legs. I wished I had the nerve to flick it off and ditch it behind some bush.

Once we got to Tommy's I mostly just held the slats of wood while Tommy hammered. He swore whenever the hammer came anywhere near his thumb. I admired this in him—girls could hardly say boo.

"Now we've got to test this table for weight," Tommy told me. He picked up the nearest object of considerable weight, which happened to be his dog, Mitzi, and set her in the middle of the table. In several slow seconds, Mitzi slid off the table onto the ground. "Mitzi, you're a joke," Tommy said. He gave Mitzi a peck on her right ear, but then I think he was embarrassed I'd seen him kiss on the dog. "Guess the table has a little slant," he mumbled. "Hand me that plane, Roxanne."

5

I reached for the plane and nearly dropped it when I heard my aunt's screechy voice assaulting us.

"Roxanne and Tommy, come in here and try this mincemeat pie!" my Aunt Ruthie hollered from the house.

"Mincemeat, yuck. Mitzi, you go in and eat it." Tommy shoved poor Mitzi gently in the direction of the house.

I let out a peal of laughter.

"Kids?" Aunt Ruthie shouted. "What's so funny?"

At dinner that night, I realized my parents weren't speaking to each other, but it was funny how long it took me to see this. I noticed some things, like how my mother wore a housecoat to the table, which she never did. Dad liked to see her in pretty dresses, enjoyed knowing they were billowing with slips from his store. My mother was wearing a shapeless broadcloth slip under her housecoat, from JCPenney. It was an old slip, from before their marriage, I knew for a fact! And the pots and pans were on the table, where typically my mother served from china bowls. Dad looked normal except that he had his sleeves rolled up. This was also unheard of. My parents were usually formal at the table, as if they were still courting, when, in fact, proof of more than twelve years sat between them.

The reason I didn't realize they weren't talking to each other was because each of them talked with great animation to me. It was a point of pride with my parents. I'd heard my mother tell friends, "Carl and I hardly ever quarrel, but when we do, we never take it out on Roxanne." I was kind of enjoying all the attention, forking biscuits onto my plate and drizzling them with honey while my parents asked me questions about my day. But not a word traveled the table between them.

Later I stood in the upstairs hallway, holding my toothbrush and listening to my parents downstairs.

"I'm on the Chamber of Commerce, Christina. The pie fair was *my* idea! And now you go and stir up trouble over *sweet potato* pie, of all things. How do you think that makes me look?"

"Mary Willis makes that pie, Carl. She's a wonderful baker. I want to see her name sitting in front of that pie when the contest rolls around, not Emma Reed's. What's so hard to understand?"

"You know as well as I do the trouble that can come of this. You got a taste of it today at your meeting. We'd like to give credit where credit is due, but—"

"Then *do* it, Carl. Maybe it seems like nothing to you, but Mary's name belongs in front of that pie. A woman bakes a little piece of herself into a pie; it means a lot . . ."

Then I heard Mom crying, and I heard no more talking. I went to my room and put on my seersucker nightgown, then realized it was still light out, nowhere near bedtime. Everything seemed a bit off, somehow. It made me feel funny that Mom was making a thing out of this pie rule situation. I wanted my parents to be like the *Father Knows Best* family. No controversies there: only lost turtles turning up in Mrs. Anderson's TV kitchen. My mother was drawing attention to us, and I didn't like it. At twelve, I felt conspicuous enough already, with my hair hanging limp and my clothes all wrong and the gap in my teeth and not even a twinge of breast showing yet. I checked once more, unbuttoning my gown. Nothing.

Now my mother was making me more noteworthy, as if it weren't embarrassing enough having a father who used the word brassiere daily in his workaday world. I wanted to disappear.

I didn't know any black girls at that time. There were only a handful at my school, and none had been in my class the year before. The black girls I saw at the park fascinated me, with their glossy kinky hair and chocolaty skin. I thought they were beautiful, but when I told a friend this once at school, she said, "What?!" and then I didn't know what to think.

The next morning I was changing into my bathing suit at the country club when I heard some girls talking about my mother's stand on this sweet potato pie thing. That's Annette for you, I thought. Everyone knows about everything.

7

"And I suppose she wants a colored queen, too, a colored Miss Cherry Pie?!" I heard one girl say.

"Next thing, we'll be swimming next to them in this pool!" said the other girl.

"Gawd!" the first one screeched.

I came around to the showers where they were and let them see I was her daughter. Before I had a chance to know I thought it, I said it. "They're people, too, you know." Then I stuck my head into the shower water for a second and stormed out, shaking hot water on whomever I passed.

Once I was submerged in cold pool water, I realized what I'd done. I'd said that to *older* girls. I began shaking, from the cold water and from my fear of what would happen when I went to school in the fall, the taunts I'd get. "Nigger lover!" And the usual: "Tomboy!" and "Hey, does your daddy sell a bra that's flat enough for you?"

That afternoon I went to the grocery store with my mother. Some people were friendly to us same as ever, but the butcher didn't trim the fat off anything, and no one helped us put the groceries in the car. When we got home Mom asked me to put the groceries away. She went to lie down on the sofa and I brought her a cool cloth for her forehead.

"Hold all my calls," she said, smiling. We had a joke where she pretended to be the president's wife, with dozens of social engagements.

"Yes, Mrs. Kennedy," I answered.

"I guess you know what's going on about Mrs. Willis's pie?" my mother asked. She took my hand.

I nodded yes and told her what had happened to me at the pool.

"Oh, honey!" she cried, clasping my fingers tightly. Her eyes filled with tears. "Well, I should have known they'd take it out on you, too. I'm so sorry, Roxie honey. Only . . . it's a lot bigger than a pie, you know?"

I felt proud of my mother at that moment. I knew then there was more to her than pies and aprons.

⋆   ⋆   ⋆

Evidently my parents had made up. When I came in for dinner that night they were back to their old selves, dressed for dinner, and animated. My mom had damp curls on her forehead from where the wet cloth had rested.

"I am renewed," she told me. "Thanks for helping with the groceries, honey."

"Roxanne," my father said, "when your mother's right, she's right." Nothing more was said about the pie fair that night.

The next day another meeting of the contest rules committee was called, and Mary Willis's pie was accepted into the fair under her own name. My mother certainly hadn't persuaded everyone Mrs. Willis deserved credit for her pie like any white woman there, but it *was* typed clearly in the rules, in the flyers that had been distributed around town. A woman bakes her own pie herself. Rules are rules.

My mother seemed to glow over the next few days before the fair, as she pulled pie after pie from the oven. Aside from the contest, pies would be sold by the slice, used in pie-eating contests, and whipped-cream ones would be used for pie-throwing games. The women of Annette were producing hundreds of pies.

And there at the eleventh hour, I finally developed an interest in pie baking. My mom was a patient teacher in those long hot days over the oven. We kept a pitcher of ice water alongside us to use in the dough to keep the butter cold, and to splash on our faces as the day got hotter. And it happened; I got the *feel* of the dough and learned how to make a decent piecrust.

"Don't overwork it now; it's tender as baby skin," Mom told me. Gently, I patted and rolled. I learned to pour the filling so that only a decorative trickle would simmer over the edge of the pie plate.

The pie fair was a success. A lot of people stopped in Annette that weekend, most on their way to someplace more exciting, but some stayed overnight and mentioned coming back to Annette one day. I didn't win the junior homemaker contest, but I did get a pale pink honorable mention ribbon for my brown sugar pie.

My mother's lemon meringue took fourth place in the main contest, and she got a silver-plated pie server engraved with her initials. Aunt Ruthie's mincemeat pie didn't place, but she won second place for her crocheted tablecloth with a red apple centerpiece. Mary Willis's sweet potato pie didn't place in the event, but many slices of her pies were bought and enjoyed.

The day after the fair, my parents and I were having ice-cream sundaes downtown at Doreen's Drugstore. There was only leftover pie for dessert at home and we were all tired of pie, so Dad suggested we go out. I sank my spoon into the thick dark chocolate at the bottom of the bowl and let the melted vanilla run over the sides of my spoon.

Doreen's husband Herbert was whacking up candy canes to make into peppermint ice cream. There was a steady tapping and then the sprinkling of pink candy on the marble countertop. He was the only person in the drugstore aside from Doreen at the front register and us there at the counter stools. The air in the store was heavy with French-fry oil and mediciny smells from the pharmacy.

"No pies to bake," my mother said, her voice surprised. She must have felt the way I did when they let us out of school in May. No homework!

We heard the bell on the front door ring, and in came Rita Cameron. She had been on the pie committee and was in Mom's bridge club. Mrs. Cameron made a beeline for the hair care section, just a few yards from the lunch counter, and picked up a bottle of blue luster shampoo. As she looked up from the shelves, her eyes met my mother's.

"Christina," she said. "Glad I ran into you."

My mother smiled and opened her mouth to say something.

"The bridge game tomorrow at Emma Reed's?" Mrs. Cameron said. "It's canceled." She pivoted on her heels and clicked her way across the store with sharp steps, to pay Doreen for the

shampoo up front. The door fell shut behind her with its cow-
bell ring.

I burst into tears. At the time, I didn't know why.

"Something wrong with her sundae?" Herbert asked.

"No," my mom said. "She's just tired. We all are. It's been a
long summer. I never baked so many pies before." Mom's eyes
misted but she wouldn't give Mrs. Cameron the satisfaction of
tears, even though Mrs. Cameron was already in her Chevy, driving home with her blue shampoo.

My mother loved bridge the way Dad and I loved baseball. I
knew the bridge game hadn't been canceled. Only my mother's
presence there had. She had had her victory with the rules committee, but there would be a price to pay; the rest of that summer
would be a bit lonely for my mom.

I didn't realize till much later that my father's business had
suffered some that summer also. Some of the ladies took their
business to neighboring towns. And so my dad, who had dreamed
up the pie fair as a boon to business, lost a little in his own store
that year. Still, he was proud of the fair. Years later we joked about
how poorly Emma Reed's dress hung on her in the photos of pie
fair events, because she shopped elsewhere for her "girdle and
whatnot," as my dad put it.

In one of those pie fair pictures, I can make out Mary Willis
in a corner, with her sweet potato pies a blaze of orange in the
picture. And my mother is the reason she's there.

Your Mail Lady

THE DAY WE FIRST SAW OUR MAIL LADY, THE FIRST MAIL LADY IN ANNETTE, TEXAS, PENNY AND I WERE SITTING out on the front porch swing, and Penny was painting her nails. It was June 3rd (I wrote it in my diary), and we were thirteen years old. Penny rested her right foot on the railing and painted her toenails with Revlon Dream Pink. Later she would have to take the polish off, as her mother had said not till ninth grade on makeup. Penny was taking pains, nonetheless, till I made the swing waver, causing a swipe of pink across her instep.

"You did that on purpose," Penny screeched.

"I did not," I said. I hadn't done it on purpose; it was an involuntary flex of the calves. I was a demon volleyball player, and those calves had a will of their own. "No one will notice," I said. We were planning to go over to Doreen's Drugstore for a Coke to get some mileage out of the polish before it came off.

Penny glared at me.

I looked at the shimmering arc of pink highlighting her foot. I actually thought it looked nice. "You'll start a new trend," I said, and at this, Penny laughed.

And our mail lady strode up the sidewalk for the first time. We had never seen her before or even heard of her, an oddity in Annette. It was 1963 and she was the only mail lady in Annette, Texas. Or in the whole county and several neighboring ones besides, my daddy said. To us, she couldn't have been more exotic if she'd worn a gourd on her head and gone bare-breasted, like the tropical women we saw in our geography book.

She was a hair under six feet tall and very thin. We could see the pull of long muscles in her arms, the rise and dip of her collarbones, shiny with sweat. She had hair the color of pecan meat, cut in a short pageboy, and she wore no makeup but coral lipstick, two bands of color against the dark tan of her face. Her blue cotton shirts gave up a smell of starch and vanilla and ink.

She walked along sorting mail in the crook of her arm. Then, leading with the arm that contained the mail for our house, she came up the steps. She was up to the box before she saw us there on the swing. I heard the whisper of paper hitting wood, and then, with the hand she'd used for our letters, she waved to us, as her palm rose to brush her hair from her face. It was hot and her bangs were damp arrows at her temples. "Morning, girls," she said.

Penny said, "Hello!" in a surprised, high-pitched voice.

I did worse. "Yeah," I said, and after she was down the steps already, "Morning." At the bottom step she paused to hitch up her left sock over her long calf. I heard the *thwack* of her mailbag hitting her hip as she did this. Then she was over next door at Mr. Breebock's in a second.

What was it about her? She seemed so unglamorous in her narrow navy skirt, her sharply pressed blouse (did she send them out to a laundry, like businessmen did?), her long black leather shoes with voluminous laces. She wore bright lipstick when everyone was wearing white-pink and her hair cut short when ponytails and beehives were in. The post office insignia was embroidered on her shirt over her right breast. It made my skin tingle to see it, as though the numbers and letters were emblazoned on her skin, a delicate arch over her nipple.

"What do you think, Roxanne?" Penny asked me, as soon as the mail lady was out of earshot.

She had beaten me to the question. In a situation like this, neither of us was willing to venture an opinion first. I hedged a bit. "Where did she come from?" As if she were from an obscure planet, at the very least.

Penny pulled a bottle of nail polish remover out of her purse,

13

and a cotton ball. She patted the remover on her striped foot tentatively, as if she expected her flesh to burst into flames or fall away like a snakeskin. "Is it okay to use this stuff on skin?" Penny wondered aloud.

The fumes from that remover were getting to me already. I had no use for the stuff. Makeup or removers. "Just wait till the full moon!" I said, clawing her knees where her pedal pushers ended. We had just seen *Werewolf in a Girl's Dormitory* at the movies. "*Whoo-ooh-ooh,* a ghoul in the school," I began to sing: the movie's theme song. I ran my nails (bare as the day I was born; no Dream Pink for me) through my hair to make a wolf hairdo. Penny laughed so hard she knocked the polish remover over, where it ate away a large spot of green paint on the porch floor. And so we avoided discussing our new crush. Our mail lady.

Not that we thought of her as a crush, of course. Crushes we had on boys. Like last fall when I gazed at Tommy Maddox's arms flexing as he worked his pen over a geometry problem. Or in the spring when I wrote Victor Antoine's name over and over in curly script on the inside of my history notebook.

Miss Swam? We thought of her as someone we admired deeply. "Yes, I admire her deeply," we said. To ourselves, to each other, or to anyone else who bothered to inquire. Miss Elizabeth Swam. It took a little detective work to come up with her full name. In the middle of June, Penny and I decided to call the operator and ask, not an easy thing to pull off in a town like Annette. "Who wants to know?" the operator gives you the feeling she wonders. Penny was elected to do it; her voice naturally rose an octave higher when she was nervous, so she didn't have to disguise it.

"Yes!" Penny screamed, when the operator asked if she could help her. "I need a phone number for a Miss Swam."

There was a mystified silence on the other end.

"The new mail carrier," Penny added.

"Oh, *her,*" the operator said, her voice brimming with disapproval. "Miss Elizabeth Swam. Eight-eight-eight, three-three, nine-

nine." She seemed dissatisfied that Miss Swam had such a musical number.

"And her address?" Penny asked. With a thumbs-up signal, I'd suggested we go for broke.

"It is not standard practice for Southwestern Bell Telephone Company to give addresses out over the telephone, ma'am."

We knew this was not really the case in Annette. Come up with a reason, any reason, and most operators would pour it out like honey on a biscuit.

"I'm calling from North Bend, where Miss Swam procures her dental services. I am Dr. Curtis B. Dim's secretary. Dr. Dim needs her address for billing purposes, and she neglected to give it to us, ma'am." Penny was trembling and pulling on her braids. She always tugged at her braids when embroiled in a massive lie.

There was a long pause. "Then why don't you call her and ask her address yourself?" the operator came back, cool as a cucumber. "This doesn't *sound* like long distance," she added.

"Ma'am, please. Dr. Dim needs me to sterilize some equipment. He is waiting in the examining room for me." Penny waved the phone at me and I made dentist drill noise, an accomplished purring buzz.

"Seven-seven-two, Misty Wood Lane," the operator snapped. She hung up.

"Seven-seven-two, Misty Wood Lane," Penny breathed, as she gently replaced the receiver. I'd heard the operator, but Penny was saying it for emphasis, to try it out in her own mouth.

"What a beautiful address," I said.

Penny gnawed on her braid contemplatively. "Do you know anyone who lives on Misty Wood?" she asked.

"The doctor who delivered me!" I said. It seemed like such a good omen.

"Doctor Dim?" Penny shrieked, giggling.

As we ran out to mount our bikes, we made dentist-drill noises, collapsing against our handlebars in fits of laughter. There was nothing that would do now except to ride over to Miss

15

Swam's house and take a look. She would still be on her mail route, so we could get our fill of the house and be gone before she returned.

Misty Wood was out a ways, a long bike ride. Halfway there, Penny said she would die if she didn't have a Coca-Cola in the next fifteen minutes. We threw our bikes on the side of the road and frantically searched our purses for dimes. Just as we were about to give up, I remembered the one in the side of my new brassiere. My mother had sewn in a dime pocket, which I had forgotten existed because I was so embarrassed I'd willed myself to forget. "Never be without a dime," was my mother's motto. A dime could buy you two boxes of feminine protection in a rest-room, or you could call home in the event of an emergency.

At Reiber's Garage we sat out back on crates to drink our sodas. Mr. Reiber was a good-looking man, if you could get past the black-smeared coveralls that bagged over his behind, the dingy undershirt you could see where his overalls zipped up to. He had a dark thatch of hair there, a whorl of it at the curve of his un-dershirt. Being close to him made me nervous, with his smell of sweat and oil, his dark brown eyes, his black hair falling over his forehead. He held his large, angular hands loose at his side when they weren't wrestling with a car part.

When Mr. Reiber found we had only one dime he gave us two Cokes anyway, beaded and steaming from the case. We must have looked a little scared, because he said, "No strings attached," as he handed them to us, then ran his huge hands in the air over the bottles to demonstrate his words. Penny and I both jumped slightly, bumping elbows and making our Cokes fizz up.

When we were perched on the crate Penny asked me, "What do you think her intimate friends call her?"

Intimate. The word was a pleasant pressure to my ears. "Liz, Beth, Libby, Betsy, Betty, Liza." I ran through the names and then took a long pull of Coke.

"Libby, I think," Penny said. "She seems like a Libby." Penny's lips formed a pout when she said the name.

"Or Beth," I said. Beth because the name was soft in my mouth like coffee cream straight off the spoon.

"How do you suppose she *got* that job?" Penny cried.

I tried to picture Miss Swam flying into the postmaster's office, taking it by storm. Among the many rumors going around about Miss Swam was that she had gotten the job by offering sexual favors to Mr. Donald, the postmaster. This was a joke though, really. Mr. Donald was sixty years old; he held little girls on his knees and fed them caramels from his gray flannel pockets, but this was the extent of his consorting with females, excluding Mrs. Donald, of course. Miss Swam was also rumored to have lost a husband in the Korean War. She wore no wedding band. She didn't wear the wistful, ironic look I would have expected of a widow.

"She has presence," I said. "Wouldn't you hire her to do anything she said she could do?"

"Yes," Penny said, putting her lips to the soda bottle to drain it.

We asked Mr. Reiber what time it was.

"Three-thirty," he said. Then, "The sun sets tonight at 8:03," he said softly.

It made my calves shiver, to hear him say that.

"We better hurry, she might be coming home soon!" I whispered to Penny.

As we raced to find the house, my purse kept slipping down and grazing my right breast, which was protected only by a camp shirt and the Kleenex-thin brassiere I wore. I thought of Miss Swam's breasts chafing against the leather strap of her mail bag.

Penny's older brother had told us that the perfect size for breasts was supposed to be what would fill a champagne glass, according to the French. We had tested this out the last time Penny slept over at my house. We snuck downstairs after my parents were asleep and eased the china cabinet open. Our nipples hovered at the top of the glasses, the tips made stiff from the cool crystal.

"Maybe he meant to where the champagne would be filled to," Penny said, giggling.

"Oooh, champagne bubbles popping," I said. *"Ma cherie!"* I cried.

"Roxie, *je t'aime, je t'aime,"* Penny whispered throatily.

Penny's brother had told us of a French movie he'd seen at the university in Austin, and Penny and I had been playing French lovers ever since.

When we got to Miss Swam's block, we set our bikes gently on the grass a few houses down and walked with theatrically casual strides over to her house. It was a small, square frame painted buttercup yellow. There was an old gray-blue Chevy in the driveway with a tabby cat asleep belly-up on the trunk.

We were furtive, as if Miss Swam's house were a library or a church. As if the neighbors would think we were planning to make off with Miss Swam's cat. There was no reason to think all of Misty Wood Lane was watching. The only person we saw on the block was an old man sleeping in a rocking chair across the street.

Penny and I got closer to the house by feigning an interest in some wisteria growing by the front steps. Showily, we inhaled the scent and murmured. From the tangle of flowers we could stand on tiptoe and glance into the window for a second. It was her living room. A blue couch, a radio, a lampshade the shape of a flying saucer is what I saw. Later, Penny told me she had seen a half-filled coffee cup on the coffee table. I wished I'd seen it; it seemed so personal. The cup had little blue flowers on it, Penny said, and the stain of Miss Swam's lipstick, a delicate curve of coral. I didn't question how she saw all this in the time she had to stand on her toes and peek; Penny had taken ballet and had strong toes.

We walked over to the car to pet Miss Swam's cat. I stroked the fur on the cat's vast belly, a silver arrow-shaped patch pointing to her chin. Penny tickled her there.

We could see the laundry line out back. A black-and-white

striped bathing suit hung by one shoulder strap and a pair of tennis
shoes dangled, the laces floating on a breeze.

On the Fourth of July, there was a big parade downtown in
the early evening, when, theoretically, it would have cooled off
slightly. I was trying to get some barbecue sauce out from under
my fingernails with a Kleenex, and Penny was fanning my neck
with a Coca-Cola sign. I'd gotten my hair cut off to the same
length as Miss Swam's hair, much to my mother's chagrin. I loved
it. Now I could really do a wolf hairdo; when my hair was sweaty
I just slithered my fingers through and it spiked up. My mother
dismissed me from the table once when I did this, but my father
laughed from behind his dinner napkin. Penny sometimes laughed
when I did it; other times she hit my shoulder blades, depending
on if she was trying to impress boys at the time.

My hair was neatly combed that night, though, because we
were going on something of a group date with a few other girls
and boys. These were the same runty-looking boys we'd been to
grade school with, who were suddenly taking on a more sophis-
ticated look. They wore clean white pants and houndstooth check
shirts. Aqua Velva wafted in the air across the parking lot as the
boys approached us. Penny and I were wearing Evening in Paris;
Penny had dabbed me with it when I wasn't looking. She also
insisted I try her lipstick—we put it on in a gas station restroom,
after our parents left Main Street. It was an iridescent pink, like
fish scales, I told Penny.

"Roxanne, ugh!" she screeched.

I was sure those boys could see our mouths clear across the
parking lot, neon lights in the dusk.

For our date, we just walked around. The boys wore white
clothes that glowed in the dark like road signs, and we girls were
dressed in seersucker dresses and skinny-strapped sandals. We
walked up and down the street, stopping to get ice cream or sodas.
Awkwardly, we separated off into couples. Penny and I agreed I
would get Eddie Feltzer and she would get Tony Martez. We

19

pivoted around on our sandals a little till this was accomplished. The boys seemed relieved we'd worked it out.

Eddie was sunburned on his ears, and his white-blond hair looked like cotton candy from being out in the sun. I thought he was cute; his eyes were smoky gray. Eddie and I talked about classes we'd take in the fall. After that, we ran out of things to say for a minute. Then I asked him what he'd done that summer, and he told me he'd mowed lawns; I looked at his arms and they had ripply blue veins from the mowing. He asked me what I'd done for the summer; I didn't want to tell him I'd helped Dad out at the store, because maybe he was one of about five people in town who didn't know my dad was the owner of Carl's Corsets. I mean, I wasn't about to tell him about folding nylon panties all summer long, so I told him about an arts and crafts class I'd taken at the Y. I asked, was he going on vacation with his family, and he said, yeah, to Colorado. We discussed skiing, though neither of us had done it, and snow. I'd only seen snow once, Eddie twice.

"The flakes are so tiny," Eddie said.

"Maybe in Colorado it clumps up," I said. "For skiing."

He laughed and tweaked my earlobe. A little wave of thrill went through me, till I saw Tony had his arm around Penny already, ahead of us. But then, my mother had said Italians were fast.

Later, Eddie and I were sitting on the hood of a Chevy by the courthouse eating vanilla ice-cream cones with chocolate shot on top, when Miss Swam walked by. She was with a woman whom I'd seen working at Woolworth's in penny candies, a divorcee, according to gossip. The Woolworth woman had her hair in a fancy upswept hairdo, but Miss Swam looked prettier in her plain page, I thought. This was the first time I'd seen Miss Swam not wearing her uniform. She wore a long red skirt and a loose, light-blue sleeveless sweater. Her arms looked especially long that night, like graceful boat oars moving through water, rather than the thick dark summer air. She was carrying a small brown sack. Did it contain chocolates? A can of tuna for her cat? A small bottle of gin? As I considered the possibilities, Miss Swam passed by without seeing Eddie and me, which was just as well. What could I say? A thin stream of ice cream started down the inside of my arm. I was glad for the darkness; I turned my head away from Eddie and lapped up the sweet, sticky vanilla with the tip of my tongue.

Then the courthouse clock chimed a quarter of nine. Nine was my curfew; we'd have to find Penny and Tony and walk home. Eddie suddenly grabbed me by the belt loop on my dress and pulled me to him. He kissed me, licking my lips a little first. Then he darted his tongue against mine a few times. It wasn't bad, but was this what Troy Donahue and Sandra Dee got all worked up about? Surely we were neglecting to do something. Eddie jumped up and grabbed my hand and pulled me off the car hood. He probably couldn't wait to get rid of a beginner kisser like me. We didn't say anything while we walked to where Tony and Penny were. We caught them making out wildly behind an oak tree: advanced kissing.

21

It was late in July, and Mom was pinning up a corduroy jumper over my knobby knees. It was too hot to be thinking of fall clothes, but she was doing it. My underwear was creeping from sweat, and my knees in the mirror looked so ugly, scraped and healed over with little red spots from shaving and from volleyball practice. I knew I would never look right. Eddie was just taking pity on me, those times he came by and walked me over to have sodas at Doreen's. Penny was going with Tony in a big way, and Eddie was just going with me because Tony was with Penny, and Tony was his best friend. Penny liked kissing; Tony even kissed her ears and neck. Eddie just poked my tongue with the tip of his. We couldn't seem to get past that. I was wondering if there was something seriously wrong with me. I sighed and ran my fingers through my hair.

"Cut it out," Mom told me. "Please, Roxanne! Just cut out the wolf stuff and act like a lady."

The screen door banged and Penny walked in with a cherry Coke in a plastic cup. Her hair was in big pink plastic rollers. She came over and let me have a sip of her drink.

"Spill it on the jumper and you're dead," my mother said, her soft tone belying her words.

I felt so bad. It seemed to me like Penny was defecting. She never wanted to play volleyball anymore with me. All she did was talk nonstop about Tony. She said she was in love, and maybe she was. She didn't want to talk about Miss Swam anymore. She told me that now she admired someone else: Natalie Wood, the movie star. Okay, but Natalie Wood did not live and work in Annette. She wasn't the first female movie star, like Miss Swam was the first mail lady. In Annette, anyway.

That night Penny slept over. To get some breeze we crept down to the back porch in our thin cotton nighties. We sat on the porch swing eating Moon Pies and drinking RC Colas. I poked my tongue into the bottle lip, practicing kissing, I told Penny. Penny didn't think it was funny. I told her it was just something goofy I'd seen my cousin Tommy do.

"Hey, Penny, I drove my bike over to Misty Wood Lane yesterday while you were at the movies with Tony. And guess what? Miss Swam's cat had her kittens."

"So?" Penny said. She had brown crumbs at the edges of her lips, Miss Perfect did.

"What, you hate kittens now?" I asked her.

She just shrugged and turned to look down the street. Looking for boys probably. She'd prance up and down the street in her see-through nightie, if boys would look.

I told her one day Miss Swam had asked me for postage due and when I put the nickel in her palm it was so soft.

"Hand cream," Penny said, "anyone can use it."

The last day of July the temperature was one hundred degrees. We stopped into Doreen's to buy a package of bobby pins, to get our hair out of our faces. As we made our way down the hair care aisle, Penny suddenly turned to me and whispered loudly, "Look, I think Miss Swam's queer." She had to tell me what it meant. "Maybe she's doing it with that woman in candy at Woolworth's," Penny said.

I couldn't say anything. I dropped my change on the floor. It hadn't occurred to me that she'd have someone. Male *or* female. I'd pictured her hanging her suit out on the line, cradling the kittens in her arms, drinking out of her blue-flowered china cup, all alone. Her life complete.

In early August, Penny and I rode our bikes out to Montgomery Ward to look at school supplies and cosmetics. Penny bought a pencil sharpener shaped like a ladybug and a Maybelline eye shadow compact with four shades of blue called "Baby Blues." I bought some gym socks and a miniature stapler. Penny was going on and on about Tony, and not paying any attention to where we were going on the way back, so I steered us along Misty Wood Lane, which was only slightly out of the way. Penny caught on when we hit the corner of Miss Swam's block.

"Rox*anne!*" she cried, giving me the look of death. "I thought you were *over* her!"

No one but my parents could say something like that and get away with it. "Go on home then. What do you need *me* for? I want to look at her kittens." I was trying not to cry. I looked over at Miss Swam's house, and saw that a light was on. She was there! Then I crashed into the back of a parked Impala. My ankle. I could feel my ankle breaking into pieces. I was thrown on my side. I shrieked, then began to cry.

"Jesus God," Penny yelled. "What have you done?" As if I'd purposely mangled myself.

We heard a door slam, and there was Miss Swam, her long white arms spread in the air. I tasted a little blood in my mouth. Miss Swam was wearing a man's shirt. Mr. Reiber came out of Miss Swam's house in his baggy gray slacks, bare-chested. They were coming over to me, and I thought, Mr. Reiber? She let his calloused fingers touch her soft skin? Her lips looked different, and I could see that her lipstick had been eaten away. I thought Mr. Reiber was going to lean over and pick me up; I saw the dark mass of hair on his chest, and felt frightened. But Miss Swam told him to go back the car out of the driveway, and he started off, with Penny following after him, babbling hysterically. And Miss Swam leaned over and picked me up in her long, strong arms that had delivered hundreds of pounds of news and threats and endearments to citizens of Annette all summer long. I smelled her vanilla smell and detected a salty scent coming from her chest. I could feel the buttons of Mr. Reiber's shirt touching my back, and I felt Miss Swam tilt me a little, so my ankle would tip up, and then she placed her large palm under my calf to support me. I fainted then.

The next day in the hospital I ate Hershey bars with almonds that Penny and Tony and Eddie brought me. Eddie stayed after for a minute and kissed me, and it was better then, as if the stillness of the hospital had given him something to rise up against.

I wanted Miss Swam to come see me, but I didn't think she would. I was only going to be there one more night. I looked at my ankle glowing white in its cast at the end of the bed and cried, because I wouldn't be a starter on the volleyball team that fall. A nurse came in with a vase of wisteria. There was a note. "Get well soon," was all it said. It was signed, "Beth Swam (Your mail lady)."

Maybe I would go with Eddie in the fall, but I wouldn't wear white lipstick to keep him. And I planned to see that my ankle was healed by home game.

The Sort of Man My Father Was

"TOM WANER! WHAT ARE YOU DOING BACK IN TOWN?"
MY MOM ASKED, HER VOICE HIGH AND PECULIAR.

I noticed she was fooling with her hair a little, patting it into place, and she even licked her lips to freshen her lipstick.

Mr. Waner was handsome, tall with brown, curly hair, like Paul Newman's, and navy blue eyes. He smelled like cologne and cigarettes.

Mom was very flustered; I'd never seen her like this. She told me she and Mr. Waner had worked together on the paper when they were in high school. Mr. Waner laughed softly. I couldn't imagine what was funny about working on the school paper. He fussed over how I looked so much like Mom.

"When I saw her, I thought she was you, and somehow the last twenty years had disappeared just like that," he said, and he snapped his fingers, a crisp loud snap that made me jump a tiny bit.

We were in JCPenney's Junior Dress Department. I went off to look at dresses while they talked. When I came back, Mr. Waner was gone and suddenly Mom was intent on our shopping; she pressed me back into the dressing room with six dresses to try on. The only one I liked she said made me look too grown-up, of course.

"I don't know what I was thinking, Roxanne," she said. "You're only fourteen."

Turned out she'd invited this Mr. Waner over for dinner.

When we got home she started polishing silver and thumbing wildly through recipe books. Finally she decided on an exotic dish with salmon and wild rice in it. Dad would hate it.

Hours before dinner Mom asked me to help her decide what to wear. I sat on Mom and Dad's bed and watched while she tried on dress after dress.

"I bet Jackie Kennedy never has this problem," Mom said. She was putting on a red crepe dress. Her face, as it emerged from the dress, was blotchy.

"What a terrible thing to say!" she said softly. "Her husband's not dead a year yet and I'm thinking about all the beautiful clothes she has." Tears started running down her face.

"Mom, you didn't mean anything by it!" I got up and hugged her, and then she sat with me on the bed for a long time holding me. She always gets really emotional about the Kennedys and starts me to crying, too.

Finally, she chose her turquoise dress with the white trim.

Mr. Waner arrived in his business suit, and Dad had changed into slacks and a sport shirt. I noticed Dad running his hands up his arms as if shocked to find them bare. Mr. Waner runs a store up in Kansas City, so Dad and Mr. Waner had a long, boring discussion about business while Mom and I set the dinner out.

"The good china—you must really rate, Tom!" Dad remarked, as we sat down to dinner.

Mom blushed, pink starting in her cheeks and ending before her cleavage, leaving her two-toned, like strawberry and vanilla ice cream.

"So, you two worked on the paper together in high school?" Dad asked Mr. Waner, as he passed him the peas.

"Yes, we sure did," Mr. Waner said.

Mom laughed a bit, looking nervous. Her eyes were bright and glittery. "It was fun!" she said, her voice high again, like it had been in Penney's. "Working on the paper."

This look came over Dad's face just then: his eyebrows arched and a very slight frown came over his mouth. *"Tom Waner,"* Dad said.

"Hmm?" Mr. Waner asked. His knife was poised butter-down over his roll.

"Oh, I just realized who you are," Dad said. "I mean . . ." He waved his hands in the air. "Christina has spoken of you before and I was just remembering . . ."

My mother's blush turned an even darker pink, making the turquoise in her dress look like neon.

And suddenly *I* realized. Mom must have gone out with Mr. Waner in high school. They hadn't just worked on the paper together, they'd dated! Now that I knew, I pictured Mom and Mr. Waner holding hands and kissing, and I had to look into my Jell-O salad fiercely to keep from giggling. Mr. Waner was handsome, with full, soft-looking lips. He could be out of a magazine. I wondered how that made my dad feel. I mean, Dad was nice-looking in his own way, but not like that. Mom, of course, was younger than Dad, and quite pretty, I thought. She pin-curled her hair into soft waves that touched her cheeks, and her eyelashes were so dark she didn't have to wear mascara. Dad talked about how pretty her ankles were. He brought home lots of high-heeled bedroom slippers for her from his store. She had them in all colors, sprawled out over her closet floor like a bed of mixed flowers.

After Mr. Waner left, Mom told me I didn't need to help with the dishes, which surprised me. I went up to my room and opened up *Gone With the Wind,* which I was about a third of the way through. I tried to figure out if Mr. Waner was more a Rhett Butler type or an Ashley Wilkes type. Rhett, I thought, but then I pictured my mom as Scarlett, swept into a passionate embrace with Mr. Waner, and I closed the book fast. I wondered if Mom and Dad were going to have an argument about Mr. Waner, and that was why they'd sent me upstairs. But downstairs all I heard was cabinets being shut, water running.

When I went down for breakfast the next day there was a note on the kitchen table from Mom saying she had gone out, but it didn't say where. My mom was always restless during the summer. During the school year she volunteered at school and served on committees, but in the summer she had too much time on her hands. Mom and Aunt Ruthie played canasta till they were sick of it. Mom experimented with her knitting, making little yarn napkin holders that collapsed into funny heaps. She tried making foreign foods, like fried cookies and flat breads. She gave these to me and my friends for snacks, and I was mortified that she no longer served them normal things like Oreos or potato chips.

When Mom came back just before lunch, she had a new hairdo, shorter and fluffier. I asked Mom if she and Dad were going to a party or something that night, but she said she'd just had a notion for something new.

Dad called to say he wouldn't be home for lunch. It was too hot to walk home, he said. My dad always walked to work because we lived so close to downtown. I wondered if he was just afraid of this weird new food Mom had been cooking. Sure enough, she made this peculiar thing out of eggplants for lunch. Mom thought a hot lunch was good for you, even if it were a hundred degrees outside.

Dad was probably at Doreen's Drugstore. All summer Doreen made this frozen salad like you get at church suppers, with whipped cream, mayonnaise, fruit cocktail, and pecans in it. On Saturdays sometimes Dad took me there for lunch and he'd have two servings of frozen salad. Just frozen salad and coffee. He swore me to secrecy since Mom would disapprove.

Dad didn't come home for lunch the next day either. He called Mom to tell her he would just grab a bite later downtown. We ate early, and then Mom sent me downtown to give Dad a catalog that had come to our house instead of the store; he needed it to make final orders on the spring line, she said. I looked for him first at Doreen's, but Doreen said he hadn't been in. I couldn't imagine anyplace else he could be eating, Annette being such a small town. The Elks Lodge maybe, but he couldn't get there on foot.

"He probably went without, because he's busy," Doreen said. "You take your dad a hunk of this here salad he loves, on the house." The frozen salad was served from a big, rectangular cake pan, and she had to warm the knife under hot water to cut the salad. She wrapped my dad's piece up on a paper plate with waxed paper.

I went over to Dad's store, but only Mrs. Windley was there. She hugged me so hard I thought my ribs would crumble. Then she asked how it felt to be a "big girl" now, meaning now that I'd started wearing a brassiere. I wanted to say, "I've been wearing them all my life, Mrs. Windley." I'd been playing dress-up with them since I was three. My mother says I used to play like the bra cups were little purses; I'd carry around puzzle pieces or tiddleywinks in them. Once I stuffed the cups with marshmallows.

Mrs. Windley didn't know where Dad was. I put the catalog on his desk and left. I still had the frozen salad with me and decided I'd better eat it so Mom wouldn't find out about Dad's habit. I sat on a crate behind the A & P grocery and unwrapped the salad. It was half melted down, and I just folded the sides up and tipped the paper plate to my mouth and let the salad slide in. The cherries and nuts were still shivery and crunchy.

When I got home, Mom didn't ask me anything about my errand, and I didn't volunteer any information. I don't know why. She set me to dusting lampshades right away, and this took me a long time because some moths had died and left tiny feelers and furry wing pieces on the lamps. While I worked I thought about how strange it was that I hadn't been able to find my father. If we'd lived in a regular-size town, there'd be all these other places downtown where my father could be eating lunch, but in Annette, Doreen's was it.

That afternoon, while Mom was at the grocery store, I put on a black satin negligee. The great thing about Dad running the lingerie store, and this almost made up for the embarrassment it caused me, was the lingerie samples he brought home. Sometimes when I had the house all to myself I'd go upstairs and try on slips and nightgowns and think up characters who would wear those things. I knew I was too old to be playing dress-up, and it made me nervous, afraid the Avon lady or someone would ring the doorbell and catch me.

This negligee reminded me of a Doris Day movie I'd seen called *Midnight Lace*. In this movie she was really scared because she thought someone was trying to murder her. It was strange seeing Doris Day in a movie like that because usually she was in comedies and musicals. She sounded so cheerful and spunky normally, but in this movie, her voice was quavery and choked with fear. The negligee was so long on me it made a pool of spidery-looking lace at my feet. I certainly didn't fill out the top part of the gown like Doris Day nor did I look a bit like her, but I willed my way into that role anyway till my skin turned pale, and my fingers and knees were shaking crazily. I caught myself in the mirror, and I had this look on my face that really scared me, because I've seen the whole movie, and I knew it was my husband who was trying to kill me! My heart beat so fast under the cool black satin it felt like it would burst through my chest and leave me empty.

The next day I told Mom I was going to meet my friend Peggy Ann downtown for lunch. She smiled and kissed my cheek and said, "Have fun. Be back by one, so you can do the groceries with me."

Of course I was really going to watch Dad, to see where he'd go during lunch. I got so hot while I walked downtown that I stopped at the library steps to take my socks off. I stowed them in my purse. I thought about calling Peggy Ann from a pay phone to tell her she was my cover, but how would I explain my mission to her? At least Peggy Ann *would* cover for me; my old best friend Penny would have sold me out in a second. I hurried on to Woolworth's, which was across the street from Dad's store. The air-conditioning prickled my skin when I stepped in. I posted myself at the window by cosmetics, so I could see when my dad left his store. I fiddled around with eye shadow samplers, painting a rainbow of blues, violets, and greens on the heel of my hand while I glanced out the window every few seconds. I'm sure the saleslady thought I was looking to steal something, the way I was acting. Finally, I bought a little mirror to show her I was okay. I almost missed seeing Dad leave. When I looked outside he was a few feet outside his store's entrance. I raced out, dropping pennies on the floor. Some spy I'd make.

Dad was about a half a block ahead of me. He stopped in front of Murray's Hardware for a minute, and I stopped in the doorway of a sporting goods store and pretended to be interested in volleyballs. I almost lost Dad for a few minutes after that; downtown was crowded at this hour. A bunch of little kids were riding hobbyhorses up and down the sidewalks, and I almost bumped into Mrs. Lawrence, who had stopped to hike up her nylons. When I spotted Dad again, he was turning in at the YMCA. My dad didn't know how to swim, and I couldn't picture him lifting weights. Maybe he was meeting Uncle Frank, or maybe a church committee was meeting there. Just then, I realized I'd better run home; it was almost one. I had blisters on my feet by the time I got home, from going sockless. My feet were tinted to the color of pumpkins, from my orange Keds.

That night at dinner, I noticed Mom and Dad had been acting kind of funny for a couple of days. Usually they were very talkative, especially at the dinner table. But tonight, like last night, we just sat there eating, only saying things like, "Pass the butter," and "Boy, was it hot today."

My mother sighed deeply. "There isn't much to do in Annette this time of year, is there?" She ran her fingernail around the edge of her dinner plate, making a tiny squeak of complaint. "Just sit and stew in our own juices."

My dad put his coffee cup down in its saucer so fast the coffee sloshed over. "Well, Christina, we can't all live in *big cities* and go to *operas* and things."

Dad was jealous of Mr. Waner! He must have been thinking that Mom was wishing she'd married Mr. Waner instead of him.

31

If she had married Mr. Waner, I'd be living in Kansas City now, going to the ballet and to concerts, like you do in a big city. I pictured myself shopping in Macy's, riding up and down the escalators. There weren't any escalators in Annette.

I might have had Mr. Waner's dark hair and eyes. I would have been very striking. But I guess it wouldn't be me. If my father had been someone else, I would have been someone else, too. Suddenly, I was glad that Mr. Waner had gone back to Kansas City; he'd told us he'd be flying back by week's end.

After dinner I saw my dad in the bathroom. He was carefully combing his hair across the top, to cover up his bald spot. We had always made fun of men on TV who did that. I thought I would burst into tears in the hallway, but I made it to my room. I cried on my chenille pillow, the tuft scratching at my eyes. What on earth had Mom been thinking when she'd invited Mr. Waner to dinner? Showing off her handsome old boyfriend in front of Dad didn't seem right, and it didn't seem like my mom. No wonder my dad wouldn't come home for lunch anymore. Maybe he was trying to track down an old girlfriend. This made my tears turn to giggles. My dad only had eyes for Mom; that I knew for sure.

The next day I followed Dad again. Once more, he turned in at the YMCA. After waiting a minute, I ducked in the door just in time to see him heading down the hallway to the swimming pool. I stopped to look at the bulletin board, looking for something that would explain why my father, who didn't swim, was heading toward the swimming pool. Like maybe the Elks club was going to buy new ropes for the pool or something; he was the treasurer. But there was no sign that would explain my father's presence there. I did notice a sign about children's swim classes; it said that adult classes were not scheduled in the summer, then it listed the times for the children's classes. One was meeting right now. Why had this brought my father down to the Y?

I went upstairs to the soundproofed observation deck. There were a few mothers there watching their children. They were

32

sharing a foil packet of roasted peanuts and drinking 7Ups. When they saw me come in, they looked like they'd been caught at something.

I sat down and watched. Several children came into the pool area, yanking at their wet swimsuit bottoms and sliding around a little on the wet tiles. Then the teacher came in and apparently yelled at them to cut it out. More children appeared, and they began to line up along the side of the pool, as the teacher directed. Suddenly, my father appeared. Incredibly, he was wearing a swimsuit, a plaid boxer-style that almost reached his knees. His hair was sticking straight out at the sides, and he wore lime-green thongs that I thought I could hear *thwack*ing against the cement as he approached the line of children. But really, you couldn't hear anything from the pool up in the observation deck.

"There he is again," one of the mothers remarked. Another woman chuckled, "Ha!" and then licked peanut salt off her fingers.

I could feel myself turning red, a slow creeping crimson starting at my earlobes, moving to my cheeks, then up to my eyebrows. Not that they had any way of knowing he was my father.

"You know who that *is,* don't you?" the salt-licking woman asked the others. "Carl Milner, who owns Carl's Corsets?"

"Oh, sure it is!" one of the mothers said. "I didn't recognize him with his hair wet."

"Why in the world do you suppose he wants to take a children's swimming class?"

Then they started talking about something else, thank heavens.

The teacher had been lecturing about something. Only my father appeared to be listening. Then they all walked down the steps into the shallow end of the pool. They put their hands on the edge of the pool and started kicking. My father had distanced himself from the children a bit, and it was easy to see why. It looked like my dad was this whale shooting up a geyser of water, while the children were little minnows spurting tiny plumes of moisture with their tails. Actually, they *were* minnows. That's what the beginning class was called; I knew, because I'd taken it when I was five.

All of a sudden, my eyes started to tear up. I was torn between horror that my dad was taking a kid's class—whatever for?—and pride that he was holding onto that tile pool edge for dear life and kicking up a storm that way: I knew he had always been scared to death of water. I imagined what his first class had been like for him, standing at the side of the pool, his hair pointing east and west, and every inch of him terrified to go into the water. I got up and dashed out of the observation deck before the mothers could see me crying.

At dinner that night I was worried Dad would be able to read in my face that I had seen him at the pool. I kept up a steady stream of chatter about *Gone With the Wind* so he wouldn't know what I was thinking about. I had just finished reading it that morning. We talked about how they were going to show the movie of it that summer in Annette, and Mom told me that she and Dad had seen it together on their third date. When it came to the middle of the movie, after Scarlett threw up the radish and said how she'd never go hungry again, the intermission lights came on, and Dad said, "Well, that was really something," and got up and put his jacket on to go. Mom had to tell him it was only intermission and there was still half to come. Dad went out to the lobby to buy a lot of jujubes and Cracker Jacks to fortify himself. If they expected people to sit in a theater for four hours they ought to feed them supper, he told Mom. Mom and Dad laughed when they told the story, and it seemed that some of the snippiness that had been in the air since Mr. Waner's visit was beginning to evaporate.

Still, I had to figure out Dad's swimming lessons. Why now? If he wanted to learn how to swim, why not wait till adult lessons were available, in the fall? And why after all these years would he decide he needed to swim, anyway? I wondered what Nancy Drew would have made of all this. But there weren't any more lunch-time spying trips for me. Mom had decided to redecorate, and she kept me busy all the time measuring windows, chipping paint, beating rugs. I couldn't slip away to the Y to see how Dad was doing. Meanwhile, Mom didn't seem aware of anything unusual, didn't notice the chlorine scent on his hair and the slight pruniness of his fingers.

In late July *Gone With the Wind* came to town. I saw it with Peggy Ann. We were smitten. Peggy Ann was for Rhett completely and thought Ashley foolish. I was torn between the two. After we saw the movie, we searched through the sea of lingerie in the guest-room closet to see if we could find a corset like what Scarlett had worn. We did; a yellowed ivory corset, brittle with bones, with a slick fabric between.

When Peggy Ann laced me into it, I could barely breathe, but I was thrilled to see that it gave me breasts. I examined myself in the oval of my parents' bedroom mirror. My white cotton panties looked all wrong with the ivory of the corset. The corset shimmered gold in the late afternoon sunlight that sizzled at the edges of the drawn shades. My hips were still flat as a boy's. I ran my hands down them, wishing I had one of those hoopskirt petticoats like Scarlett's that would fashion me into a woman. The kind Rhett would stare at with his dark eyes, his mouth curled with pleasure.

Then Peggy Ann tried on the corset. She had breasts even without the corset's help, and she looked very grown-up in it. She had the most wonderful hair, too; it wasn't fair. It was red as could be and very fluffy. When I brushed it, it felt like a cloud of fur there, like something alive in my hands. She had a beautiful dusting of freckles, too (which she hated), and milky skin. Still, *I* had Scarlett's green eyes. That was something.

While we were putting all the lingerie back in the closet, I knocked a little shoe box off a shelf in the back. A bunch of photos and notes fell out, spilling all over the place. Peggy Ann grabbed one and said, "Wow, Roxanne, was your dad this cute before he got bald and everything?"

"He is not *bald*, Peggy Ann." She could really make me mad

sometimes. I looked at the picture and knew right away it was Mr. Waner back when he was in school with Mom, but I just said it was a cousin of Mom's and got Peggy Ann to go downstairs with me for Cokes on the back porch.

As soon as she left, I ran back up to the closet to dig the box back out and looked at the picture of Mr. Waner. He was even more handsome then, with liquid, dark eyes and those full, soft lips, and hair slicked silken, parted at the side. On the back of the picture it said, "To my beautiful Tina, all my love. Always, Tom."

I'd never heard anyone call her Tina. She always went by her full name. And *love always*?

Now I knew why Mom had been so flustered when she'd run into Mr. Waner at Penney's. I wondered what had come between them all those years ago. I looked at the other pictures; most were photos of other high school girls, but I did find a picture of Mom and Mr. Waner together, dressed up for a dance, it looked like. Mom wore a dress with a heart-shaped bodice, and she had long wavy hair to her shoulders. Her head was thrown back, and she looked like she was laughing. Mr. Waner was dressed in a baggy suit, which made him look very thin, and he had on the narrowest tie I've ever seen. His full lips looked dark in the black-and-white shadows.

As I was putting everything back in the box, I noticed a picture of the boys' swim team. There was a tiny arrow over one of the boys. Mr. Waner, of course. Slick with swim water and pointing a finger jauntily at the camera. I hadn't thought about my father's swimming lessons for a couple of weeks, but suddenly the image of him in his plaid trunks, his hair awry, came to me as clear as a snapshot. I knew why he had started swimming lessons just after Mr. Waner's visit.

The next day Mom and I were hemming some new curtains for my room, and the photo of Mr. Waner and Mom dressed up for the dance came into my mind. I wanted to ask Mom if she still had that dress, but I thought she'd be angry I had poked through her photos and things. If she *had* saved the dress, would it mean she was still a tiny bit in love with him?

"Do you ever wish you'd married Mr. Waner, Mom?"

"Married Tom?!" my mother asked. A little fan of sewing pins rested on the edge of her lips. She pulled them out and placed them at intervals in the hem before saying anything else. "What an idea! No, no, he was just my high school boyfriend. He was a lot of fun, but not half the man your father is."

Over the next few days I thought a lot about just that: the sort of man my father was. He was a shy man, with the unlikely job of lingerie salesman. He was not a natural athlete, like Mr. Waner, but he was the biggest armchair baseball fan ever. He was crazy about my mother; from her flower bed of bedroom slippers, to the way he hung on her every word, I could tell. I had even seen him kissing her hair once, when they didn't know I was looking. This seemed very romantic, to me. Maybe Dad didn't provide me with big-city thrills, like Mr. Waner might have, but he was a dad who was there for me always, ready to play Monopoly, to explain algebra, to take me to lunch at Doreen's. A man who ate frozen salad on the sly.

In early August we set off on our summer vacation. We were going to San Antonio so I could see the Alamo. We'd spend a night there, then drive down to Corpus Christi. After we'd driven for about three hours or so, we stopped in Austin for some ice cream, and Dad suggested we drive over to Barton Springs, a swimming pool fed by natural spring water. At first we were just going to take a look at the pool, but it shimmered so crisp and cool we couldn't resist a dip. Dad said it was okay, we were in no hurry, which surprised Mom and me. Dad usually kept us on a tight schedule, even on vacation.

When Mom and I came out of the dressing room, we looked over in the concession area for Dad, expecting to see him taking it easy, drinking a Coke while he waited. He wasn't there. We looked out over the springs, at the angular rock formations surrounding the water, the dark green branches that cast speckled shadows on the surface. There was Dad, walking into the water, looking dashing in a new burgundy swimsuit. The water parted before him as if it had done so a hundred times before. My mother's face was stirred by many emotions during those seconds. First, a smile, to see Dad wading. Of course, she would assume it was only a bit of wading. Then a look of terror when she saw he meant to go under. What in the world? her face asked. Then we both watched my father swim the most beautiful strokes we'd ever seen. My mother's head tipped back and her lips parted in a jubilant laugh. "Carl, you rascal!" my mother squealed. And she was in the water swimming toward him.

You Never Know

"THE LORD WORKS IN MYSTERIOUS WAYS," MY MOTHER SAID. SHE HAD JUST TOLD ME SHE WAS PREGNANT.

Funny, this subject had come up at an end-of-school-year slumber party at Lucy Baker's the weekend before. We had been speculating on whether or not our parents still "did it," while we combed and styled each other's hair. My new best friend, Sue Ellen, lit into me with a rattail comb.

"Mine, no way," Sue Ellen had said.

She'd teased my bangs till they sprang up over my forehead like fur. My scalp tingled. "Mine either."

"Even though your dad runs that lingerie shop?" Lucy asked. She tipped her head back to hurl some popcorn into her mouth, careful not to smear her lipstick.

My father's line of work had always been an embarrassment to me, but now that I was fifteen, I was just getting the total picture. I took a French-blue, scalloped-cup brassiere from my dad's store once when he wasn't looking. Wearing it beneath my crisp, bleached white camp shirts, I felt like Brigitte Bardot. Still, I didn't want to associate any of this with my father, let alone my mother.

"Just because he sells the stuff . . ." I'd retorted feebly.

But now here was my mom with irrefutable proof nestled inside her. I was mortified. Sure, when I was young, I had wished for a brother or sister, but after all this time? This was 1965, and people had their children in intervals of two years. Everyone did.

"Your father and I always wanted another baby," my mother explained. She was bustling around the kitchen like always, filling pots, chopping onions. "It just never happened," she murmured.

You'd think they'd been going at it gangbusters, the way she talks, I thought. Here I'd been waging battles to get Mom to treat me like an adult, but now I wanted to be her baby again, the only one. Tears rolled down my face, but she didn't know I was crying till she asked me to bring her some potatoes, and I didn't answer.

"Oh, honey," she cried.

She came over to me and pressed my face to her stomach, and I smelled vanilla on her apron. I listened to her stomach like the baby in there might say something to me.

"You're still my baby, Roxie. My first baby and my only Roxanne," Mom told me. A pot boiled over on the stove then, and she let go of me, to see to it.

It was the end of May when I found out about the baby. I decided to get a summer job, so I wouldn't have to hang around the house listening to Mom and Dad talk about the new baby all the time.

In a town as small as Annette, Texas, there wasn't a lot to pick from, summer job–wise: counter girl at Jerry's Dairy King, shampoo girl at Babs's Tint 'n' Clip . . . but then I heard about the maid job at the Bluebonnet Motel. At a motel, I imagined I would meet all kinds of people: traveling salesmen, journalists, gypsies! These people would know the *world*. I pictured myself dressed up like a French maid, wearing a black uniform made of some slick, filmy fabric, with a little white lace collar.

I sat in the manager's office for the interview. There were dented boxes marked Sanitize Strips, stacks of stained towels, even some rusty sink stoppers set on the windowsill as if for decoration. The whole time Mr. Oatman spoke to me he lettered small pink cards with, "Thanks! Come again next time

you're in Annette!" Later, my friends would die laughing at
this.

I got the job and was put to work directly.

"Put it on, sugar pie," Hannah, the head maid, told me. "Ain't
nobody here but us." Hannah was a squat woman who looked to
be fiftyish. Her salt-and-pepper hair was knotted up with what
looked like a dust rag.

Reluctantly, I undid my skirt zipper and pulled off my top.

"Some brassiere!" Hannah remarked.

"My dad owns Carl's Corsets," I said. The grayish mauve uniform settled onto me clammily, looking puckered and askew in
the mirror no matter how I smoothed it.

"It won't lay flat, sugar. It's crummy material," Hannah said.
"So if your dad *owns* a business, how come you're here slumming
at the Bluebonnet? You can't get enough money for Cokes and
junk from the old man?"

"I'm saving for a car. Plus, I want to get some experience," I
said.

"Well, there's plenty of that here, honey doll. You plan on
working in them heels? You'll teeter into the john when you clean
the thing."

I knew then that this job wasn't going to be as glamorous
as I'd hoped, but I was determined. "I didn't bring any spare
shoes."

Hannah gestured toward a pile of shoes in the corner of the
dressing room. "Roxanne, you wouldn't believe how many people
are so stupid they don't even check under the bed when they leave
their motel room. Try those yellow sneakers."

I followed Hannah from room to room. She pushed the cart
of cleaning stuff, and I dragged the heavy vacuum cleaner. Once
we were in a room, Hannah would click on the TV, pull the
bedspread up over the dirty sheets on the bed, and lie down to
watch soap operas. She instructed me in my duties while she
watched her shows. "Wash the john first. Then it has time to dry

so you can put on your Sanitize Strip without its dissolving." I
could vacuum only during commercials. When her story came
back on, she shouted "Whoa!" indignantly, and I raced to flick the
vacuum switch off.

I did most of the work, but Hannah spritzed and wiped the
TV screens and helped me strip and make the beds. In one of the
beds we found some tiny black bikini panties. Crotchless.

"Your pop sell stuff like this?" Hannah asked.

"Certainly not!" I cried.

"Mr. Oatman will get a kick out of these," Hannah snickered.
She put the bikini in her pocket.

"You're giving them to him?"

" 'Less you want 'em, honey doll." She threw the panties at me.

They fell onto my foot, looking like a large spider there. I
kicked them back over to Hannah. "I'm not that kind of a girl," I
told her.

"No, you're not," she agreed. "Let's go to the coffee shop
after this one."

After break, we went to clean room 27. A tiny sign posted
beneath the room number said EDWARD FRED, ACCOUNTANT. Hannah knocked on the door.

"Mr. Oatman lets him run a business in here?" I asked.

"Sort of," Hannah answered. "He gets business downtown,
but he does the work here."

Hannah used her passkey to let us in. There were stacks of
books and papers, a whole closet full of clothes and shoes, drawers
filled with things.

"Why does he live here?" I asked Hannah.

"The rooming houses are full," Hannah said. "Leastways,
that's what he *says*. He's been staying here for a month."

The bed was made neat as a pin. We stripped it and put the
clean sheets on, but somehow it had looked tidier the way he'd
done it.

"Army man, must have been," Hannah said. Since there were

no soap operas on this late in the afternoon, she helped me clean the room.

Having someone's shoes and soap and things to move around while we cleaned gave the room a whole different feeling. Like cleaning a real home. "Where does he come from?" I asked.

"Philadelphia," Hannah told me.

"Why in the world did he come here?" I wanted to know.

"Nobody knows," Hannah answered.

In Annette, if anyone knew, everyone did.

Hannah sat me down on the fresh-made bed. "A word to the wise, miss. Sometimes, once you're cleaning by yourself, he'll be here when you knock. He always gets his papers together and goes to the coffee shop to work, when I've come to clean. But if he ever stays around for a bit, while you're here alone with him, watch yourself. He's all by hisself here in Annette, and he's always been a gentleman to me, but you never know . . . he's a man, and men have their *needs*. And, well he's an odd bird, you know?"

I didn't know, but I took in her meaning. I'd think about it later.

Saturday morning at the drugstore, my friends and I drank lemon Cokes, and the five of us shared one small order of French fries. We were on a diet. I reported on the things I'd seen at the motel: *Playboys*, garters, crotchless panties. We were giggling over this last when the soda boy, a freshman, brought over a dish of lemon slices to add to our Cokes. Marcy had complained they weren't sour enough.

"What's so funny?" the soda boy, Denny, asked. His mouth was curved and tensed, ready to laugh along.

"You're too young to hear about it!" Sue Ellen practically screamed. We were going to be sophomores, and felt worlds older.

Denny turned pink at his hairline. "Oh really," he muttered. He took a piece of lemon from the dish and ate it right down with no sugar or anything. The peel even. His whole face turned pink as he tried to keep his lips from puckering.

"Wow," I said.

Denny smiled at me, then went back behind the counter to make a milk shake.

"Denny likes you," Sue Ellen told me.

"He's too young. You said so yourself," I answered. I could feel my chest getting speckled. It always did that when I got embarrassed.

"He's cute, though," Lucy commented.

"Shh!" I told her. "He'll hear you." Despite the fact the milk shake machine was roaring. To divert them, I told them about my mom's pregnancy.

"Jesus, Roxanne," Sue Ellen said. "When it turns fifteen, you'll be—"

"Thirty," I said. "I know."

This sank in slowly. We ate up the fries, even the small burnt pieces.

"So your parents do it!" Marcy whispered noisily.

"I guess so," I said. I was so speckled I was sure they could see the pink dots right through the thin cotton shirt I wore. "I guess so."

My dad was going bald, and my mom had a few gray hairs, and they were having a baby. What good would a baby brother or sister do me now? It wasn't like we could be buddies or anything, with the gap in our ages. And my social life was sure to go down the tubes once I had to baby-sit all the time. Still, I tried to act excited, for their sake. When I got home from Doreen's, my mom was going through a box marked "Roxanne, Baby" that Dad had dragged down from the attic for her.

"Look at this, Roxie," my mom said, in a singsong voice. She was dangling a pair of booties made out of flannel. They were the color of baby aspirin, an orange pink.

"My feet were that little?" I asked.

"You bet they were," Mom answered. She slipped one of them over her thumb. Mom took out a little dress next, with puff sleeves and smocking on the front. It had little yellow ducks all over it.

"I remember that!" I said. But I couldn't really remember that far back, surely. "Or I guess I—"

"You've seen it in snapshots, honey. It was your favorite. Duck was one of the first words you learned. Right after mama, dada, and *no!*"

She handed the dress to me. The white collar had yellowed a bit, but the dress was still pretty. And it was soft as could be next to my cheek. I could smell a faint baby smell, even with the smell of mothballs mixing me up. "Baby smell," I said.

"It's like a good French perfume," Mom said. "It just hangs on forever and ever."

"I can't believe you saved all this stuff. You really did want another baby, all this time?"

"Even if I hadn't, I would have saved these, Roxie. But yes."

Monday, when I went to the motel coffee shop for lunch, I noticed a skinny man in the back booth; he was wearing a long-sleeved shirt and dress pants. He had dozens of papers spread out on the table. He must be Mr. Fred, the accountant, I thought. His necktie was loosened, and it was hovering over his coffee cup, about to dip in. "Watch out for your necktie," I told him.

He seemed extremely startled to be spoken to. His head jerked up, and his pen clattered onto his coffee saucer. I could see he was wondering if I was another waitress. Their uniforms weren't much different from ours. "I'm a maid here at the Bluebonnet," I told him. "My name's Roxanne."

"Please sit down, Miss Roxanne. I'm Edward Fred. I'm pleased to meet you." His skin pinkened to the color of cream after strawberries have been sitting in it. Which reminded me of Denny at the drugstore, both of them blushers.

I hesitated for a minute, thinking about Hannah's cautionary words. But what did Hannah know about him really? I sat down across from him. "I can only stay a minute. I'm meeting my friend Sue Ellen here for lunch."

"I see," he said. "How nice to have a friend to meet for lunch!" he exclaimed. He made it sound pretty out of the ordinary.

"You're new in Annette?" I asked.

"Yes, I am," Mr. Fred said. "Coffee, Miss Roxanne?"

"I guess I could have a cup. Sue Ellen's always late."

Mr. Fred snapped his fingers to get the waitress's attention, and pointed to his coffee cup, then me. You could see he was from the east, that way. No one clicked their fingers for service here.

"Don't worry, you'll get to know everybody," I told Mr. Fred. "This town's so little-bitty it's a joke."

"I like it," Mr. Fred said. He tucked his tie into his shirt when the waitress poured him a fresh cup of coffee.

"Sure, I like it, too," I said. "But I want to live someplace bigger someday. You from a big city?"

"Chicago," he sighed.

"Oh?" I said. Everyone says Philadelphia, I wanted to say.

"The 'windy city,' it's called. And that's what it is," Mr. Fred said.

I stared at him as I nodded. I couldn't figure out how old he was. His sandy brown hair was thinning a bit, and his eyelashes and eyebrows had gone completely gray. His eyes were very blue, which should have made him handsome, but he had thick-rimmed glasses on, which nobody looks good in. And he looked scared. Not just nervous. Scared. Not of me, just of everything.

"Still," I said, "there are a million things to do in a big city." I saw Sue Ellen pull up in the parking lot in her dad's pickup. "My friend's here," I said. "How much do I owe you for the coffee?"

"Not a penny, Roxanne. It's on me. And thanks for doing my room up so nice every day. And for talking to me today."

"Sure thing, Mr. Fred." I got up.

"Call me Ed," he said softly. He smiled and turned pink all over again.

As soon as Sue Ellen and I sat down at the other end of the coffee shop she asked me, "Who *is* that guy?"

I told her about him, what little I knew. We ordered a BLT to split and a vanilla milk shake, to split also.

"I've seen him walking around downtown a few times," Sue Ellen said. "He always wears a long-sleeved shirt, even when it's over a hundred degrees he does. And he doesn't roll up his sleeves, isn't that strange?"

"I guess so," I answered.

"How old is he?"

"Well, I didn't ask him! Gawd, Sue Ellen."

"He could be almost as old as our parents," Sue Ellen said. "And he bought you a cup of coffee!"

"Sue Ellen, that doesn't exactly make it a date or anything, you know."

I noticed Mr. Fred gathering up all his papers. As he passed our table on his way out, he stopped for a second and said, "Girls, you're not eating enough." He went up to pay and then left. A minute later the waitress brought us hot fudge sundaes.

I told the waitress we hadn't ordered them, and she said, "They're on Mr. Fred."

"He really likes you, Roxanne," Sue Ellen said, in her taunting tone. "But Roxanne, he's too old!"

"He's too old for me; Denny's too young. I know, I know."

"Roxanne, did you say he told you, 'Call me Ed'?" Sue Ellen screeched. "Ed Fred! *Ed Fred!*" She giggled in that high-pitched way of hers that drove me crazy.

"Don't laugh at him," I told her. I licked some fudge off my spoon. I missed my old friend Peggy Ann; she had moved to Dallas at the end of our school year. She would have understood.

I should have knocked longer on the door, I realized too late. I came in on Mr. Fred in his undershirt. He had slacks on, too, but in the context of a motel room, he looked almost naked. His arms were glued to his sides; they were skinny and muscular, like Steve McQueen's in the movies.

"Oh, whoops!" I cried. I tried to back the cleaning cart out of the room too fast, and it caught on the doorjamb and teetered. Windex bottles and rags fell off the cart. "I'm sorry," I said.

He ran to help me, and as he bent to pick up a bottle off the floor I saw his wrists. There were long red scars all up and down his wrists. He saw me looking and ran to put on a shirt. Long sleeves: no wonder he wore them all the time. It took a few seconds to register. An accident, I thought, at first. His arms scraped along the pavement somehow. But I knew it was no accident with scars like that. I couldn't move. I stood there, and Mr. Fred picked up all the bottles and rags and placed them carefully onto the cart.

"Miss Roxanne," he said. "I'm sorry. I should have put a DO NOT DISTURB out. I'm running a little late today."

For the first time in my life I was literally speechless. I just looked at Mr. Fred. He had tried to kill himself.

"Here, sit down please," Mr. Fred whispered. He helped me to a chair. I could hardly bend my knees to sit.

"Your . . ." I murmured. I touched the palms of his hands. They were soft. And just inches from the slashes.

"Well," Mr. Fred said, "I'm sorry you had to see such a thing. It's not a very pretty thing for a nice girl like yourself to see, is it?" He perched on the edge of the bed, then stood up again. "Let me get you a glass of water."

The water brought my voice back. "I never knew anyone who . . ." I waved my hand slightly, making the water slosh over.

"Don't worry, dear, it's not contagious." He said this softly.

"Why did you do it?" I asked. "It's none of my business, I know."

"Roxanne, you have a family, am I right?"

"Of course."

"Brothers, sisters?"

"Well, my mom's carrying one."

"How lucky for you, Roxanne!"

"Maybe." I still didn't see it.

"You have a family. You'll never be alone."

"You're lonely."

"Not so much as I was in Chicago. Funny thing how more people makes you more alone. But yes."

I heard Hannah hollering for me outside; I had a lot of rooms to get to. I told Mr. Fred good-bye, then pushed my cleaning cart through the door, with Mr. Fred assisting me over the doorjamb. Mr. Fred's cool breath smelled of Clorets.

All I could think about was how to make friends for Mr. Fred. He was a nice man, and he looked good except for those glasses. He was a little odd, kind of formal or something. Or maybe it was just being here in Annette. Any stranger stuck out extra strange. I thought about bringing him home to dinner sometime. But what would I say? Mom and Dad, I met this guy at the motel? Their worst fears would get fanned up. Especially with my feeling of desperation showing. Feed this man dinner, be his friend, or *he might kill himself!*

After dinner that night I went upstairs to soak my feet for a while. I poured some lilac bath crystals into the water. Mom had given them to me out of the blue, fancy stuff wrapped in gold foil with French words on the label. She knew I was still having doubts about having a baby brother or sister at my age, and she was trying to woo me. Baby pictures of me materialized around the house: me with hardly a scrap of hair on my head, tummy down in a dishpan bath, grinning. Me, two years old, with my fist stuck into my birthday cake. Stuff like that. I remained skeptical. "Will I have to change its diapers?" I asked.

"After a few times, you'll think nothing of it," she assured me.

I was ruminating on dirty diapers and Mr. Fred's loneliness when the phone rang. Dad called me to the phone. It was Denny calling to ask me out. I didn't know what to think. He was cute, but what would Sue Ellen think of me going out with a freshman? Not that I cared much, but . . . I was thinking about this and meanwhile hemming and hawing to Denny over the phone.

49

"Okay, I get it," he said. "You don't have to let me down easy."

"No, I mean I'm just tired tonight," I told him. "I'm on my feet all day, and—"

"Yeah, sure," Denny said.

"Okay, I'll go," I told him.

I had to get ready real fast, and I nicked my ankle to pieces shaving too quick. There was a thin trickle of blood into the bathwater, and I thought of Mr. Fred's wrists and felt so bad I got to crying. I had to put a washcloth over my face to calm down, then I had to redo all my eye makeup and be someone's date all of a sudden.

50

We saw *The Pink Panther* at the Grenada Theater downtown. I was surprised Denny was able to pick me up, his being fourteen, but his family lived outside of town, so he had a rural driving permit. The car was a blue Oldsmobile; it used to be his granddad's, Denny told me; it was sky blue and had a big-boat feel to it. My parents waved good-bye from the door. This was my third real date, not including the group dates I went on when I was a kid. My parents weren't too comfortable with the idea yet. Daddy would wait up for me; Mom would want to, but the pregnancy made her sleepy.

The movie was really funny. I was a little self-conscious laughing out loud in front of Denny; how did my mouth look when I was laughing? I'd have to check in a mirror sometime. He was laughing a lot, too, and his mouth looked great, his lips soft. I thought of his lips puckering from the lemon at Doreen's, and I laughed at Peter Sellers and Denny both.

After the movie Denny drove me out to the lake. I knew it was a make-out spot, though I'd never been there. We held hands and talked about the movie. We had some Junior Mints leftover from the movie, but they'd melted to the bottom of the box. Denny got a plastic spoon from the glove compartment and spooned the chocolate out for me. His feeding me like that seemed sweet at first, but then I thought, that's how you feed a baby, and started to worry again about how everything would change when my mother had the baby. All of a sudden, Denny began to kiss me. He was a good kisser. My skin tingled beneath his fingers, buzzed even; I felt like me, Roxanne. I had kissed only two other boys before this, and they'd kissed like it could be any girl there pressed up against the dark car upholstery.

Because of what Mr. Fred had said about being alone, I didn't feel like letting go of Denny, once we were together like that. I let him press against me in a way I'd never let another boy do, to feel for sure that I was alive over each and every inch of my skin. I felt the snap of his jeans press into my thigh, I smelled the saltiness of his neck, and tasted chocolate mint in our mouths. Outside the car, fireflies flipped on and off like sparks of electricity, and I heard a few restless fish in the lake flop up and splash back in. Denny's hair was short and springy in my hands. I drank in every little detail.

"Your eyes look purple at night," Denny said.

"You've got me mixed up with Elizabeth Taylor," I told him. Flattery from boys usually made me think, what do they want from me? but I didn't feel that way with Denny at all.

All at once it occurred to me that I was old enough to have a baby myself. I mean, I knew it before, but it just that minute sank in. I knew it could happen in cars. And did. Just imagine, I thought. If I had a baby it would grow up right along with the baby my mom was having, and my mom would be mom and grandma to two little babies all at once. My baby's aunt or uncle would be the same age as my baby. I told Denny we'd better go home.

I'd started cleaning motel rooms by myself now; Hannah and I split the rooms up. I talked to myself while I worked. The morning after my date with Denny, I thought about him a lot. I lay down on the motel beds after I made them and thought about what it would be like to be on a bed with a boy. With Denny. Of course I wasn't planning to do it. But I could think about it. I could close my eyes and his face would swim up, his skin soft and tanned to the color of vanilla mixed with caramel. His eyes were set far apart, but I couldn't remember what color they were. And after his comment about mine being purple at night! I remembered how I liked his body's weight against mine.

But then I would switch into these other thoughts. About getting pregnant. I knew I was too young. And my mom was too old. My parents did that! That's what I couldn't get over, that they had pressed against each other like Denny and I had, that they had felt some of the same things. I couldn't believe that my parents could have feelings like that.

As I spritzed the mirrors with Windex, I would see myself come into focus again and again, and each time I was startled by how I looked. Older, somehow, as if I had done it. I knew a girl at school who had, and she looked like this a little, older around the eyes and lips. Like a woman. Was it all a feeling, having nothing to do with years or what you had done?

When I got to Mr. Fred's room, he let me in himself. I told him I could come back later, but he told me he had something to show me. "Here, sit down," he said. He took my arms and led me to the bed and sat me down on it like he'd done the other day when I was in shock about his wrists. What else could he have to show me, after that? "Close your eyes," he said.

I closed them, but all I could think about was what Hannah had said, about how men have needs. I didn't want to think that, not about Mr. Fred. He was lonely, but not like that. But then I thought, if my own father has needs . . . God, anybody could. I got really scared; I felt like Mr. Fred was going to show me his thing. I heard a zipping sound. God, he was unzipping his pants.

Then he said, "Put out your hand."

He was going to put his thing in my hand! I didn't put out my hand. My hand was on my lap. All of a sudden, I felt something hairy on my palm. I screamed and jumped up. But it was just this tiny kitten. It dropped to the floor when I jumped up. I scooped the kitten up and began to pet and kiss her. I felt like a fool.

"What did you think it was?" Mr. Fred asked.

"The fur surprised me, that it was something alive," I lied. I couldn't believe I'd thought that about Mr. Fred.

"I'm sorry I scared you," he said.

She was a beautiful kitten, gray with darker gray stripes and big green eyes. I saw a canvas bag on the floor with big holes punched in it. That's where the kitten had been. He'd unzipped it to take her out.

"It's for you," Mr. Fred said. "It's a little friend for you, since you've been a friend to me."

"Oh, Mr. Fred!" I started to cry. I was all worked up about everything. Here he was a person with so much sadness in his life he'd tried to kill himself, yet he was so generous and kind. "Mr. Fred, you'd never try to kill yourself again, would you?"

"I don't think so, Roxanne. Probably not."

Just *probably*, I thought! What could I do, I had to figure out a way to make sure he would never try it again.

Just then, Mr. Oatman burst through the door. "Hannah heard you scream. What's going on in here?"

"Nothing, Mr. Oatman," I told him. "I just dropped the vacuum on my foot." I couldn't tell him what had really happened; I hardly knew myself.

He looked at my feet in disbelief. Then he turned to Mr. Fred. Mr. Oatman had a look on his face like he'd seen Mr. Fred sprout a third arm. He seemed torn between accusing Mr. Fred of something and wanting to keep his only regular customer. "What's with the cat?" Mr. Oatman asked.

The kitten must have thought she was hiding under the bed, but her long tail twitched in plain view.

"No pets allowed," Mr. Oatman said.

"She's mine," I told Mr. Oatman.

When I brought home the kitten after work that night, I was surprised to find that my parents had no objection. We had never owned a pet before, but Dad told me he'd had a terrier named

Mr. Bone when he was young, and that he'd loved it like a brother. It was when Mr. Bone died and broke my father's heart that he'd vowed *never again*, and he'd stuck it out until now. But when I came in with the kitten, they said okay. I named her Millie.

They told me she was my responsibility completely. I carried her around the house with me all the time, kissing her and telling her my problems. She was beautiful. Her ears were sloped to a high tip, and she had a trace of yellow pointing to the sky. She could do anything. She jumped onto my stomach in the bathtub and got her feet only the slightest bit moist. I thought, Mr. Fred should have kept her, he's the lonely one. But already, in such a short time, I loved her so much myself. And the day before, I'd had no notion of wanting a kitten.

54

My next date with Denny was at the drugstore, after closing. Denny had the key. It was fun being there in secret, but what if Doreen or Herbert, the owners, came back for something? We had to leave the lights off, of course; we went to a booth in the back and sat in shadows holding hands and necking. It seemed so strange to be in this store in the dark, this store I'd been going to all my life. It looked so different at night with the shampoo and mouthwash bottles glowing red and green and blue, the ice-cream freezer humming and shivering. Denny made me a milk shake, and the machine seemed to be making a delirious racket in the quiet of the night, like it was funneling extra electricity into itself from the moon and the stars. Denny told the machine, "Shh," and we got to giggling. I giggled till tears ran down my cheeks, then cried in earnest.

"What's wrong?" Denny asked me. He poured the milk shake into a glass and brought it over like it was medicine I must take immediately.

I told him about everything. About my mom being pregnant so old, about Mr. Fred's slashed wrists hiding beneath his long sleeves, about Mr. Oatman and Hannah, how cynical they were about people. I told Denny about all the stuff people left behind in motel rooms, the rubbers and crotchless panties: how first it was exciting seeing it all, then just sleazy. I talked about my kitten, Millie, how I'd only had her a couple of days but already I was crazy for her. And I told Denny I liked him so much, but what would people think in the fall at school, him a freshman and me a sophomore. "I just have a lot on my mind," I told him.

I was embarrassed he'd seen me cry. I knew my makeup was all down my face in streaks and that my lips had that quivery look they get when I cry. "I must look awful. I don't know why I worry so much about everything."

Denny wrapped himself around me, and we curled up there together in the booth. "It's just the way you are. I like the way you are."

55

The next day when I went to clean Mr. Fred's room, before I got out the passkey, I saw his drapes were open. Through the window, I could see him on his bed. Still asleep at 2:30 in the afternoon? But he had all his clothes on. Then I saw a pill bottle on the bedside table. It was knocked over, with a couple of pills spilled out, glowing yellow in the sunlight. And his arm was drooped off the bed in a funny way, and his mouth looked so slack!

I screamed so loud my eardrums hurt. I saw Mr. Fred sit bolt upright, his hair literally standing on end. I screamed again. I thought he was waking from the dead.

Mr. Oatman came running over and so did Hannah, and Mr. Fred came to the door and unlocked it. We all stood and looked at each other in confusion.

"I saw that bottle of pills," I told Mr. Fred. "I thought you'd killed yourself."

"I get migraines," Mr. Fred said. "Those are headache pills."

"You scared me!" I shouted. I began to cry. Hannah held me against her massive chest and patted my head.

"I'm sorry I scared you, Roxanne; I'm so sorry," Mr. Fred said softly.

"You two are bad for business," Mr. Oatman said. "Little girl," he told me, "you're fired. And, Mr. Fred, you're out. That's it."

At first I thought this was so unfair, but then I felt relieved. Mr. Fred needed a better place to live and work. And I needed a more restful job, for sure.

The rest of the summer went by as slow as always, after that first speeded-up part. I worked for Dad at his lingerie store. He let me help up front sometimes, and it was fun knowing what half the women of Annette wore under their clothes. Mrs. Smoodler from church wore a longline bra. My old kindergarten teacher, Miss Snow, wore boy-leg cotton panties. I tried predicting what people would wear underneath their clothes the moment they walked through the store entrance. It made the summer move faster, though August still seemed months long to me. I longed for the cool of fall; I was dying to wear a sweater. This was a change for me; as a kid I'd always wanted the summer to last forever.

Dad's store was close to the drugstore, so I got to see Denny during every break. I had to watch my figure, with all the ice cream he was feeding me. Nights, at the lake, we held on fast to each other. When it looked like we might go too far, we got out of the car and walked into the cold lake up to our knees. Even if the other kids at school thought he was too young, I knew Denny was the one for me.

Sue Ellen and I got to be better friends. She told me Denny was really cute; she'd only made fun of his age because she was jealous. By the end of the summer, we were double-dating.

Mr. Fred got a room at a boarding house. I visited once a week or so, and he told me about plays he'd seen in Chicago and fixed me grilled cheese sandwiches he made by wrapping bread and cheese in tin foil and running an iron over them. He still wore long-sleeved shirts all the time around town, but when I visited he rolled up his sleeves. After a while I got used to seeing his wrists and forgot to worry all the time that he might try to kill himself again.

Over the rest of the summer, I stopped screaming and crying all the time. There was no point to carrying on; it only
wore me out and made the summer even hotter than it already
was. I had sweet Millie to play with. She might get run over
and break my heart, but I could only hope not. And I came to
think, sure I might hate my baby brother or sister come winter,
when it arrived. But on the other hand, I might love it to
pieces. You never know.

Angel Food

W HEN I GOT GREAT-AUNT ADELE'S OLD STEAMER TRUNK OUT TO PACK CLOTHES FOR COLLEGE, MY MOTHER started sneezing wildly: *heh-choo-oo-ooo-it!* We were a family with distinctive sneezes: Dad sneezed, *hehchoova,* I sneezed *het-shue,* and little two-and-a-half-year-old Joanie, *hisshue.*

The trunk was covered in half an inch of soft feathery dust, decorated with small spider carcasses and paw prints from my cat, Millie. I banished Mom from the attic till I had it cleaned up. Daddy brought me a bucket of Spic and Span and supervised the cleaning. This meant he ate pistachio nuts and told stories of his college days.

"Of course, I participated in very few panty raids," Daddy said.

Very few! But by the time I opened my mouth to inquire, Daddy was on the topic of dormitory food.

"Roxanne, if it's Salisbury steak, take my advice and run for it. Here's a few dollars for you to get you a Whataburger when the occasion arises." He stuffed what I later found to be three fifties into my pants pocket. I polished the pale green metal lid of the trunk. Daddy grabbed a chamois and buffed it.

"Pretty as a picture," he said. My daddy liked a job well done. "My baby going to college." He kissed my cheek; his pistachio breath smelled sweet.

Then we searched for a solid hour for the trunk key. We finally called my cousin Tommy in on the job, because he had uncanny finding abilities. Sure enough, within ten minutes, he had it. He refused to tell us where he'd found it, though Joanie mounted his chest and pummeled it to get the story out of him. (I told her to.) He bronco-bucked her, sending her into fits of giggles, till Mom screamed out, "Tommy, lay off or that child will wet you!"

To celebrate the finding of the key, we ate Eskimo Pies on a blanket on the lawn. Joanie wore so much of her pie on her face that Tommy's dog, Mitzi, ran to her and licked her all over. Mom stripped Joanie down to her pink cotton panties, the ones that said Tuesday on them, even though it was Friday. Daddy left to go back to work, and Joanie and Mom went upstairs to take a nap. Tommy and I climbed up to the attic to examine the contents of the trunk. Mom had given me some cartons to put Aunt Adele's things into; she said she'd go through them later.

"Aunt Adele was who? Some chick who went across the ocean, I guess. Look at all these stickers." Tommy often answered his own questions.

"My mom's aunt. She got to go to Europe her junior year of college."

"Is she the one who died last year?"

"Yeah, that was her. Remember when we drove to Dallas after Thanksgiving? That was for her funeral."

It surprised me that Mom hadn't looked in the trunk since it had been shipped to our house. I pulled out some linen dresses and blouses. They were tea-colored and had a few delicate moth bites here and there, but I thought I might wear them anyway. I was wearing a halter top and bell-bottoms; I took one of the dresses and let it fall, soft and swirling with dust, over my head.

"Groovy," Tommy said. "You look like that chick who sang 'To Sir with Love.' "

"If you wanted the moon, I would tie it up for you . . . " I sang.

"Whoa! I didn't say you sounded like her."

"You take it off me; I'm afraid I'll rip it." I put my arms up in the air like Joanie did for me to undress her.

59

"What makes you think I'm so good at taking dresses off girls?" Tommy asked, smirking.

"Ha ha."

It was hot as heck up in the attic, even with the exhaust fan noisily clattering air at us. Tommy's hair was sticking up from when he'd run his hands through it, and it was spiked with glittery sweat.

We got back to work. I spotted a cigar box full of photos. I wanted to look, but Tommy was already getting bored. There was a box of fossilized peanut brittle. I found a Dutch butter cookie tin that had what looked to be a hundred buttons in it. Wood, pearl, glass, crystalline. It looked like treasure Joanie would enjoy. I found a little jewelry box with a pink butterfly brooch in it.

"Ug-a-ly!" Tommy said. "My mom would love it, though," he added.

It was true that Aunt Ruthie would love it. I told him to take it for her. There was a shoe box of letters, which I saved to put under my bed so I could read them at night. We put everything else in cartons and carried the trunk downstairs to my room.

That night at dinner a little battle sprang up between my parents. Apparently, my father had forgotten the pinochle game they were to host the next night and had scheduled inventory for the same time as the card game.

"Why can't you reschedule it?" Mom pleaded. She was cutting Joanie's steak up, and she was so peeved with Dad that she cut it into teeny bits. It looked like hamburger meat. Joanie stirred the bits into her mashed potatoes.

"Honey, if it was just me. But Doris and Ethel are planning to stay late for me, and I hired Tommy and Rox to help, and besides, it's the last night I can do it and still meet . . ."

"We have three couples coming over for pinochle! I will not call and cancel this late."

"You know I always do inventory the third Saturday in—"

"All right!" Mom drank off her iced tea like it was a stiff drink.

Joanie popped a cherry tomato in her mouth, and when she bit it, juice and seeds shot out over the whole tablecloth.

Mom gave Dad and me a look that made it clear our lives were in danger if we laughed. Meanwhile, Joanie burst into tears.

"Baby-pie, it was an accident, don't worry. Roxanne, take her upstairs and give her a bath now."

My mother began to clear the dishes furiously, and actually took Dad's plate while he had a bite of food in midair. "Carl, you will have to call everyone and cancel."

She couldn't have devised a worse punishment for my father, who disliked social telephone calls and hardly ever used the phone at home.

Up in the bathroom, I ran a tub of warm water and let Joanie pour in a capful of Mr. Bubble. After stripping her, I lowered her into the bathtub. As I lifted her hair to scrub her back, she asked me a question: "Mommy and Daddy mad?"

"Yeah, a little, honey, but they aren't mad at you. Don't worry. Tomorrow they won't be mad anymore."

I kissed Joanie's hair, the little part of it that wasn't damp yet. It was incredible to me that three years ago I had been unsure whether I wanted a sibling. She had turned all our lives upside down, but in a good way.

I poured a dollop of Baby Magic shampoo into my hands, then soaped Joanie's hair gently. I sang "When You Wish Upon a Star" to her. She hummed along in her sweet off-key voice.

Later in the evening, my mother and I were carrying Cokes into the living room to watch Carol Burnett on TV. We heard Daddy in the den on the phone telling the Nickersons that Mom had a sick headache and he didn't think she'd be up to the pinochle party the next night.

I could see Mom trembling. The Coke bottles clinked together, then one slid to the floor. It didn't break, but a foamy brown pool formed at our feet. "Poop!" my mother shouted, the worst curse my mom could muster.

"What happened?" Daddy asked. He came to the door of the den.

"Sick-headed me, I just couldn't hold onto the bottles," Mom whispered furiously.

"Christina . . ."

Mom stomped upstairs and left Daddy and me in the sea of Coke foam. I went to get a mop and when I came back, Mom had a stack of sheets and a pillow, which she heaved at Dad.

"I guess my head is a bit too sick for having anyone in bed with me tonight," she told him. So Daddy was to sleep on the couch in his study that night. This occurred five or six times a year.

In the living room, I peeled back the cocoon of foil from a pan of Jiffy Pop, and I watched television. After all these years, my parents' fights still shook me up; experience showed me they would make up, but I worried what Joanie would think after I left for college when Mom and Dad had fights, without me there to reassure her. I remembered the time Mom and I took the bus to Dallas and stayed at Grandma and Grandpa's house for a few nights, till she forgave Daddy. I was seven at the time and feared that my life in my hometown, Annette, was over, that I would have to invent a new life with Mom and Grandma and Grandpa in Dallas. Dallas was a big, scary city. Every night I had wrapped myself in blankets like a mummy and tried to reconcile myself to nights without Daddy's good-night kiss. But the truth was I couldn't sleep right without that kiss; I had suffered from complicated nightmares that involved running off cliffs, like Wylie Coyote.

Carol Burnett's Tarzan yell brought me out of my reverie. I licked popcorn salt off my fingers and stretched out on the couch. Maybe I would talk to Mom and Dad about letting Joanie see them kiss and make up, too. That was always a sight to see, since in truth they were crazy about each other. Their feelings—all of them—just ran high for each other.

I lay in bed that night sucking on Tootsie Pops and reading Great-Aunt Adele's letters. There was a packet of love letters from a Chet Zimolski tied in a pink ribbon. In all the letters there was one long paragraph about the war (he was stateside and had desk duty, but he described how terrible the food was, chipped beef especially, as if to show he suffered, too) and then a few rhapsodic words of love. Each letter ended, "You still haven't answered, sweetcake, will you be my wife?" It was a question that extended itself over many months.

Great-Aunt Adele was a knockout in her time; I had seen photos of her as a young girl. Sometimes my mother said I looked like her, and this seemed high praise. I wondered if my future held any boys in Nam poised on rice paddies, writing begging letters to me, suffering worse indignities than chipped beef or unsurety of my love. Aunt Adele had long hair she wore plaited, and though I had known her older, when her hair was spiked with gray, as a young woman, her hair color had been mine, a nutmeg brown. Her eyes were lake green like mine, and her hands delicate and long-fingered. I examined my fingers as they held a glistening purple Tootsie Pop aloft. Suddenly I was sleepy. I went to sleep with my teeth coated with sticky purple.

63

Despite Dad's excuse for canceling the card party, Mom still didn't have a sick headache the next day, but a real reason for canceling the party had come up: Joanie sprouted chicken pox all up and down her arms. "Lord help me," my mother said.

She must have been remembering my bout with chicken pox when I was five, which at the time, Doctor Redman said was the worst he'd seen in a decade. Mom sent Daddy to the drugstore for calamine lotion, some coloring books, penny candy, and a few pints of Lady Borden ice cream. Our family believed ice cream cured anything.

"Lucky thing is, with Joanie only two and a half, she'll barely remember this when she gets older," Mom said. She scratched her own arm for a second, a sympathy itch for Joanie, no doubt.

"Not like me! I'll never forget a single miserable, scratchy moment of that summer," I answered.

"Why do you girls always get the chicken pox in the summer!" Mom asked. She poured a cup of coffee for me and one for herself, and then we forked bites of Sara Lee coffee cake directly out of the aluminum foil pan. The fact that my finicky mother didn't even bother to get out plates showed her state of mind, I believed.

Joanie, who had been watching *Captain Kangaroo* in the den, toddled out to the kitchen and looked at us, a feverish brow raised. She scratched furiously at her arms, then wet the floor.

My mother laid her head on her arms momentarily. "This will undo her potty training," she murmured.

I carried Joanie upstairs to change her, while Mom mopped up. Here was one thing I wouldn't miss when I went to college: the smell of pee-soaked cotton.

A half hour later, I parked Joanie on the divan in front of the TV again. The divan was swathed in cotton sheets, and Joanie wore pink and white seersucker jammies and a large quantity of calamine. I put a bowl of vanilla ice cream in her hands, and then Mom and Daddy and I ate bowls of ice cream in the kitchen with coffee. Crippling our teeth with steaming hot and arctic cold, we fortified ourselves for the long day of illness and inventory ahead. Mom and Dad seemed to have made up. Daddy had bought her a little box of Russell Stover chocolates at the drugstore as an "I'm sorry" gift.

After an early dinner of tuna sandwiches, Daddy and I drove to the store. Mrs. Windley was just closing up. I helped her with the day's receipts while Daddy prepared for inventory. Tommy arrived and began horsing around with the mannequins; he did this whenever he had the chance. "Fly me to the moon, and let me dance among the stars," he crooned. He danced with the mannequin we'd named Monique, swirling her chiffon negligee behind her. Next, he put underarm dress shields up to his ears and pretended they were Mickey Mouse ears. "Minnie, come give me some sugar!" he hollered in Mickey's high-pitched voice. He seemed like a ten-year-old when he acted like this, though in fact he'd turned eighteen last month.

At 6 P.M. Daddy locked the door and we began inventory. Though the store's name was Carl's Corsets, in '68 our big seller was soft bras, bras that were almost not there at all. Daddy called them Kleenex brassieres. I was up to my elbows in shivery pink chiffon when my old boyfriend Marvin called. He had been my date at the prom, and I had broken up with him soon afterward. It was a breakup of convenience, for the most part; he was going to college up north, and I didn't want to spend the next four years carrying a torch for him. He was brokenhearted, then he was mad at me. I sent him copies of our prom picture in June, and he sent them back to me "Return to Sender." He had gotten a job in Dallas for the summer, a two-hour drive from Annette, but he drove back to town every night. I hadn't even seen him once since we'd broken up, which is hard to pull off in a town tiny as Annette. But now here he was on the phone begging me to go out with him that night.

"I can't even if I wanted to," I told him. "I'm doing inventory." Tommy had paused from his work to smoke a cigarette, which he had to smoke right next to me and the phone, naturally. He was the one who had answered the phone, and he knew exactly what was going on. He smiled crookedly at me and, with his price gun, stuck clearance tags up my left arm. I tried to clobber him with a stapler.

"Even if you wanted to. Uh huh," Marvin said.

He sounded so sad. I closed my eyes and remembered things Marvin and I had done together. After months of scrambling around the backseat of his Mustang, we had driven to a Motel 6 in Dallas one night last year during Christmas vacation, and we had done it. My first time. His second. Then we had done it and done it, up till a week after the prom, when I broke up with him.

"Well, I want to," I surprised myself by saying, "but I'm doing inventory."

"Meet me afterwards," Marvin said softly. Begging was becoming to him; it wasn't to all boys.

"It would be about midnight," I told him.

*   *   *

In the bathroom at the back of the store I put on Love's Shimmer Pink lipstick and thanked my lucky stars that I had kept taking my birth control pills, though I hadn't had sex with anyone since Marvin. Daddy wouldn't exactly approve of a date that started at midnight, so Tommy was my cover. I told Daddy we were going swimming at the lake, and off we went. Two blocks from the store, Tommy dropped me off at Marvin's Mustang. Marvin and I drove one more block, stopped the car, and started messing around. I was struck with wonderment that I had broken off with Marvin. He was combing his hair a new way and he was wearing a different cologne, too, something mysterious and dark and potent. Was this Marvin or his evil twin, I wondered, as my Kleenex bra slid off my breasts and Marvin unzipped my jeans a fast zip, and I, his, faster. My panties were halfway down my thigh when I heard a distinct rap on the windshield. I had thought the flashing lights were a part of lovemaking with the new Marvin. But no. It was the police. If the lights worked, why didn't the siren? Marvin and I pulled on our clothes in record time. We got out of the car and saw the policeman was Larry Fenster. His son Rafe had been my debate partner when I was a junior. Officer Fenster ran his flashlight up and down us. We stood braced against a car door. Marvin held onto my pinkie finger; I would remember that always.

"Kids, kids, kids," Officer Fenster bellowed. Then he whispered, "Ya'll even know where you are?"

I couldn't make sense of this question. It seemed big and philosophical. Marvin was equally dumbstruck. Officer Fenster pointed skyward. I noticed the cross then. And a glowing Virgin Mary who glowered at us.

"Now, kids, I know ya'll are Protestants, but do you think this is any way to be acting here?"

Marvin piped up, "No, sir."

"Er, no, sir," I echoed.

"Let's you kids and I take a little ride in the old blue and white, shall we?"

This sent shivers done my spine. I was scared of police cars. Could he throw us in jail for messing around by the Catholic church?

"Sir, we promise we will never ever—" Marvin begged.

"Get in the car, son. You, too, Roxanne," Larry Fenster ordered.

We got in the police car, and Officer Fenster drove us to the highway, away from town and the police station. Marvin and I were too scared to say anything. What would the charges be? Would we spend the night in jail? I was terrified of jail. On TV, they always had rats, and I was scared of rats worse than anything. Equally scary was the idea of my mom, all worn out from Joanie's illness, or Dad, exhausted from inventory, coming down to the station to spring me from jail.

Ten minutes outside of town, Officer Fenster pulled up at the make-out point by the lake. I sensed dozens of couples scrambling in their respective cars. But Officer Fenster only said, "Don't ya'll know *this* is where to go to do it?" He laughed heartily, then turned around and drove us back to Marvin's car. Jesus. Marvin and I clasped hands in the dark backseat. Officer Fenster talked about the recent Fourth of July parade, the new grill cook at Doreen's Drugstore, the price of cantaloupe at the Minimax, and four or five other things. We chatted politely with him. When he dropped us off at Marvin's car, he said, "I don't believe I'll be calling your parents on this. Night now."

Marvin and I drove to Jerry's Dairy King and ordered chocolate-dipped cones. We argued about whether "I don't believe I'll be calling your parents" meant for sure that he wouldn't. Marvin was convinced he might; I was convinced he wouldn't. But we ended the evening with a trip to Honey Lake: just following Officer Fenster's orders.

The next morning Joanie looked like she had been splatter-painted in pink. Right after breakfast I was sent out for more coloring books, candies, and some medication Dr. Redman had prescribed. When I got back I went up to my room and took out some more of Aunt Adele's letters. I had run out of ones from Chet Zimolski.

Down in the kitchen I got myself a bottle of Coke. It was early in the day for a Coca-Cola, my mom pointed out, but I hadn't gotten much sleep last night (which I wouldn't point out to her; mercifully, all were sound asleep when I'd returned from my date last night). I took the letters and my soda out back to the glider swing. The sky was a shimmering purple; it was going to rain, finally. I loved summer rain. I read a letter from a Mabel Piereen to my Aunt Adele. "Darling," it began. My teeth clinked against the Coke bottle lip. "I long to unsnap each snap of your uniform with my teeth and to run my fingertips under the rise of your breast beneath your, I am certain, pale rose-pink brassiere, and to nibble your tender lower lip, and—" Wow! What in the heck? Who was this *Mabel?*

A clap of thunder bounced me off the swing. I tucked the letter into my back pocket and looked to the heavens to see a bank of clouds rollicking by, and then large dollops of rain began to fall. For a moment I sat on the swing and let myself get polka-dotted with rain. Then I ran inside, skidding on a patch of wet dirt, till I tumbled into the kitchen, breathless and damp. Mom was lifting a spice cake from the oven, redolent of cloves and allspice. Daddy's favorite: a sure sign they'd made up.

I sprinted upstairs and changed into a dry T-shirt and cutoffs.

"Roxanne, pudding, dip your sister in calamine again, won't you?" Mom shouted softly up the stairs.

That night when I got the letters out again, I found eight more from Mabel. They had worked together at a factory during the war. Mabel had quite the eye for Aunt Adele, it seemed. And from the tenor of the letters, it seemed clear to me that Adele had returned the sentiments. I closed my eyes and thought of Aunt Adele the last time I'd seen her. Her hair had been piled up in a wild mountain of silver and burnished brown, and her lips had been painted fuchsia pink by one of the attendants at the home who was studying cosmetology. The residents were all gaily painted, and it was a bit like going to the carnival, going there. That day she spoke of her childhood, the time she spilled lemonade all over her good church dress and got a walloping from her daddy. The time she sang "Oh Promise Me" at the wedding of a girlhood friend who "had" to get married.

Aunt Adele had never married, I knew that. I wondered if any of the family knew about her.

The next day my parents were preparing for the pinochle game, which had ultimately been bumped to Monday. Mom rolled cocktail peanuts in seasoned salt, and Daddy stocked the refrigerator with Coke and 7Up, and the liquor cabinet with bourbon and scotch. Joanie was still speckled, but a bit less inflamed. I would be in charge of her tonight while Mom and Dad entertained.

Later I'd go to the store to help Daddy out, but for now I went to meet my friend Sue Ellen for breakfast at the Hi-Ho Cafe, a greasy spoon at the edge of town. Best friends since we were freshmen, we had planned on going to the same college all through high school, but it didn't work out that way. She would be going to Our Lady of the Lake in San Antonio, and I was going to the University of Texas in Austin. I would miss her like crazy.

Sue Ellen had sprayed Sun-In hair lightener on her reddish brown hair and now had zags of orange stripes. "You know me and chemical experiments," she said. She bit into her fried-egg sandwich, and egg yolk shot down her chin.

Did I. We had nearly burned down the chemistry lab last spring. It kept us both off the honor roll. I laughed while I curlicued syrup onto my hotcakes. Sue Ellen told me her parents were letting her take the miniature refrigerator from their houseboat to school with her in the fall.

I had spent many happy moments on that houseboat, mostly clandestine. Sue Ellen and I would drive out there after dark. The boat always smelled like grilled hamburgers because Sue Ellen's family ate them every Sunday night when the weather was good. Her family hardly ever took the boat out on Honey Lake; it was just parked on the edge of the lake, for the kids to swim off of, and to fish occasionally. We'd had many parties there, Sue Ellen and me, and a handful of our friends. Sue Ellen and I had skinny-dipped there dozens of times. I'd never forget the first time I took the lake between my bare legs.

Thinking of this brought Great-Aunt Adele's letters to my mind. "Sue Ellen," I said. "I guess you never met my Aunt Adele? She was my mom's aunt; she worked in a factory during the war, and she never married. My mom inherited her trunk when she died last year, and I found this bundle of love letters in there."

"Anything juicy?" Sue Ellen asked. She frowned at her empty coffee cup.

"Well, as a matter of fact. Some of them were from a guy named Chet Zimolski, pleading with her to marry him. But she wasn't interested . . . in him, anyway. The others were from a Ma-bel Piereen. She was in love with Aunt Adele, too."

"A woman!" Sue Ellen stopped skating her toast crust around in the yolk puddle on her plate.

"Yup."

"Jesus, Roxanne. That's something. Is it weird reading what she wrote? Were they steamy?"

"Pretty much. It's weird putting it together with the Aunt Adele I knew, but the stuff she wrote was, I don't know . . . sweet and dirty at the same time."

"Sweet and dirty. Hey, that should have been our prom theme!"

We both snickered. The waitress brought us coffee from a fresh pot. My fingers shook from caffeine, but it was a feeling I liked.

"I'm going to miss you, Sue Ellen."

During the pinochle game that night, Joanie and I sat outside on the glider and looked up at the stars. She was so smart I was teaching her the constellations, while other tots learned kitty and red and ball. "Don't scratch, little bunny," I told her. Her chicken pox was getting better but still itched her.

She laid her head back in my lap. "Wittle dipper," she said.

I straightened her pajama collar. The seersucker's crisp stripes felt good between my fingertips. Joanie's hair tickled my bare thighs. Her hair was dark, like Daddy's. In the night light I saw that her bangs were a thumb's length (her thumb) from her brows. Would I need to trim them before I left for college? I couldn't find a way to explain to Joanie about going away to college. She knew I was going away, but she didn't know what going away was. I always cut Joanie's hair. Could it wait between vacations? She was too young for me to go away. A tear slid down my face and landed on Joanie's cheek.

"It's raining!" Joanie cried.

I held her tiny feet in my hands; they still fit in my palms.

"Oh, just one," she said.

"One what, honey?"

"One rain."

The next morning Mom told me Daddy had gone to the store already, and that he didn't need me to work that day. She suggested we go downtown and pick up some things I'd need for school. Aunt Ruthie had offered to keep Joanie.

We bought a hot plate and a small iron and a folding ironing board. Also cardigans and jumpers and knee-socks: Mom hoped I'd dress like that at college. I put some jeans and T-shirts in the pile, and she paid for all of it.

We were walking to Doreen's for lunch and I thought, it's now or never. "Mom?"

"Yes, dear?" Mom shifted her shopping bag from one hand to the other.

"When I go away, if you and Daddy fight, be sure Joanie sees you make up, too, okay?"

"You think it scares her?" Mom dropped her shopping bag.

"It did me."

"I didn't realize—"

I picked up Mom's shopping bag and carried it. I looped my arm around hers. "Mom, don't feel bad. I saw how you made up. As long as she sees that, she'll be fine. I just worry about her, with me not around."

"She'll miss you bundles. We all will, baby. What will we do without our Roxanne?"

"I'll miss you, too."

At Doreen's we had bacon burgers and potato chips and milk shakes. We talked about the courses I would take in the fall at school. My parents had decided finally that I could take the old Malibu down to school, and Mom was already worrying about where I'd park on campus. She dropped her straw into her milk shake and I watched it sink into the thick chocolate foam.

Mom pulled a *Cosmopolitan* out of her purse and gave it to me. "You might want to read this," she said. She'd dog-eared an article titled "Contraceptive Methods: Which One Is Right for You?"

I spurted a bit of milk shake onto the table.

"Of course, I am not advocating premarital sex, Roxanne. But Austin is a big city, and well, I read things. So when the time comes . . ."

I said nothing and stuffed a lot of chips into my mouth. "Uh, thanks." It seemed best not to explain about the Pill. I had gone to Dallas with Marvin after Christmas last year to a doctor named Schmeedman, who gave me the spiraling packet of pills in a hot pink case. *Cosmopolitan* indeed: my mother.

This new development gave me the courage to mention Aunt Adele. "You know, Mom, I've been reading Aunt Adele's letters."

"Really? I don't know if I approve of that. Letters are private, Roxanne."

"Well, but she didn't throw them out."

"No, I guess—"

"There are a bunch of love letters to Aunt Adele from a woman, Mom!"

My mother's eyebrows flared slightly. But she didn't look too surprised, really. She mouthed, "Cup of coffee," to our waitress.

"You knew?" I asked.

"Yes and no. I mean, I think it must be one of those things you know deep down. As soon as you said it, I could see it."

"You're not shocked?"

"I don't know. The price of ground chuck shocks me. Dick Nixon getting on the ticket shocks me. But matters of the heart . . . no. What was the woman's name?"

"Mabel Piereen."

"Mabel Piereen! Gosh, I remember when Daddy and I were first married we went to Thanksgiving at Aunt Adele's. I made this red Jell-O salad that never jelled. With fruit cocktail in it. It was soup. Anyway, Mabel was there. I think that was her name. She was a very tall lady with frizzy hair who was Adele's house-guest. Imagine that. She made the most delicious angel food cake with dark chocolate sauce poured over."

"So, do you feel funny about it?"

"Angel food?"

"No, Mom, Aunt Adele."

"Oh. No, I don't somehow." Mom stirred cream into her coffee and tapped the saucer a few times with her spoon. "I'm happy she was loved."

Marvin called me that night. "Roxie, *je t'aime*," was all he had to say. Mom was right. It was good to be loved. By a chicken-pox-cranky mom or an inventory-exhausted dad or a pee-pantied sister. By a sweaty-haired cousin who would love me from afar; Tommy had just received his draft notice. By a best friend with streaks of fire in her hair who would be just eighty minutes down the highway from me in Austin. By Marvin, even, who would worry about Officer Fenster's dialing finger for his last few weeks in Annette. Who would worry about me from a few thousand miles away, while he kicked snow off his boots in Chicago and I wore sundresses in December in Texas. It *was* good to be loved.

Solace

THAT SUMMER IT SEEMED TO ME THAT MY MOTHER WAS TRYING TO FILL UP THE EMPTY SPACE IN HER BEDROOM closet that my father had left when he died. For it was then that she became a compulsive shopper, cramming the closet with new clothes, their crisp fat tags jostling together when sleeves met.

Just as I was finishing finals at the end of my second year in college, my aunt phoned to say that Mom had fainted in a Neiman Marcus dressing room in Dallas; she was shopping so hard she had forgotten to eat lunch.

"Roxanne," Aunt Ruthie's voice boomed over the telephone line. "Why on God's green earth does your mother need so many clothes? You should see her closet, it's a scandal! Your mother even has coral-colored shoes, can you believe it?"

I couldn't agree with Aunt Ruthie that coral shoes were scandalous, but the fainting worried me. I had been planning to stay in Austin for the summer, but I decided to return to my home-town, Annette, instead, to keep an eye on Mom and Joanie, and to help Uncle Frank at the store.

My first day home, Mom sent me off to the pool with my four-year-old sister, Joanie. While I was putting zinc oxide on her nose, Joanie let slip that Mom slept all the time now, when she wasn't shopping. I asked her what she did while Mom was asleep.

"I play Barbie dolls or watch cartoons. I don't mind."

Joanie's hair had already drawn tiny tracks in the white cream on her nose.

"Dive in," I told her.

It was just an expression; Joanie didn't know how to dive yet. I jumped in next to her and enjoyed her look of surprise when we both emerged from the frigid water into the sunlight.

My mother must have known that Aunt Ruthie had ratted on her about the shopping, because when we got back from swimming, Mom was in the closet trying to conceal some of her purchases. I knocked on her bedroom door and heard a lot of tissue paper rustling and the sound of shoe boxes falling. As I opened the door, she shrieked.

"Mom, for chrissakes, it's just me!"

She jumped out of her closet, stumbling over shoes. "Something was moving in there!"

Joanie had followed me into the room. "A mouse!" Joanie screamed; she jumped up onto my mother's bed and hopped around, dripping pool water onto my mother's good chenille spread.

I peered into the closet, ruing the fact that I had no older brother. "Get me a flashlight," I intoned, like Dr. Welby on TV asking for a medical instrument. Mom ran off to get a flashlight, and Joanie continued jumping around on the bed screaming. I stepped out of the closet and grabbed her by her shoulders. "Shuhh tup!"

Mom came back with the flashlight and told Joanie to go take off her suit. The next thing we knew Joanie was back, nude and pale with chill, her wet hair slapping around her shoulders as she resumed jumping around on the bed.

"Put on some *panties!*" my mother shouted.

If my Uncle Frank had been at the house he would have installed Mother in the living room with a tall Tom Collins and soothed Joanie with some lemon drops and RC Cola. My family believed mightily in sugar as solace. But Uncle Frank wasn't here; Daddy wasn't here. I was left to take care of this. "Stand back," I told them.

75

We had never had mice before. "Don't be a mouse, don't be a mouse," I whispered. More likely than not, the intruder was a tree roach. In Texas they were almost as big as mice sometimes, and they'd fly right at you. This was why women still sometimes wore hats inside. Once my cousin Tommy had scared Joanie by claiming that a Milk Dud on the movie theater floor was a tree roach; my sister never touched a Milk Dud again.

As I investigated, Mom's clothes slithered over my bare back and arms. The ones that still had tags on them somehow gave me the creeps (they felt like wings or little feet). Suddenly out of the corner of my eye, I saw something move. "Shit!"

"Roxanne!" my mother reproached. "Little pitchers have big ears!" Ever since Joanie had made her way into the world, I had been hearing this.

Then, "What is it?!" Mom asked. "It's not a mouse."

I didn't know what it was. I told them it was nothing, just a shadow. Joanie, bored with hopping, climbed down from the bed and told me she thought she'd go outside and jump rope.

"Put some clothes on first," my mom and I both said at the same time. She rolled her eyes at us, then left the room.

Mom went down to the kitchen to start dinner while I stood looking at all the clothes in Mom's closet. Aunt Ruthie was right; this was crazy. I counted five pairs of red shoes alone. There were dresses of all colors and styles, even some gold Capri pants, which was something my mother would never in a million years wear. When I reached out to touch the fabric, a tiny pink toe curled around the price tag dangling from the waistband. A gecko darted around the tag. I screamed and leaped up and bonked my head on the closet rod. Now I knew what people meant when they talked about seeing stars: tiny gold dots bounced around. I bit my lip and hurt all the more. I could hear my mother's mules punc-tuating each stair with a click, and then she was there helping me out of the closet.

Down in the kitchen, my mother gave me a steak to put on my forehead. The meat felt cool and moist, but my head still throbbed. I was crying, which I hadn't done in front of my mother in a long time.

"Honey, you'll make yourself sick!" Mom said. The next thing I knew she stood before me with a Miller High Life. I thought she meant for me to replace the steak with it to cool my head, but she said, "Go on, drink it." I had heard those words so many times over a dose of vile medicine that I hesitated.

My mother flipped the cap off and I heard it roll around the linoleum. I began to drink the beer.

"I know it's not your first," she murmured. She reclaimed the steak, rinsed it, drenched it in Worcestershire and put it on the broiler.

"Did you find something in the closet?" She'd asked so softly you'd think I was going to announce the bogeyman. Or maybe the bill collector, judging by the closet's contents.

"It was a gecko."

My mother turned, aghast. Her potato masher dripped a dollop of hot potato onto her foot, and she jumped. "What's a gecko?" she asked, suspecting the worst, it seemed.

"It's a little teeny lizard," I told her.

She looked suspiciously into her colander of string beans, like one might become animated suddenly. "Here, string these," she told me.

I liked the crisp snap and the way they tasted cold and raw. I drained my High Life and wanted another but didn't dare ask. "He looked kind of sweet," I ventured.

"Sweet?!" my mother cried out. "How do we get rid of it? If your father were here, he'd know what to do."

My father had died last Thanksgiving. My mother and Aunt Ruthie and I were swathing Thanksgiving leftovers in Saran wrap down in the kitchen when it happened. We heard a loud thump upstairs, and we all stopped in our tracks. My Uncle Frank dropped the saucepan he'd been washing into the sink. He was wearing a frilly yellow apron to keep the turkey drippings off his sailboat necktie while he washed dishes. We had all teased him about it, before. Joanie had fallen asleep at the dining table, her little face collecting Parker roll crumbs from the blue linen tablecloth. Uncle Frank told us to stay put, and he bounded up the stairs. There he found my father crumpled by the bed, like he'd meant to have a lie-down. But no. His heart had done him in.

He was only fifty-nine. The doctors discovered an odd, minuscule defect in his heart afterward. Something that couldn't have been detected before, we were assured. This was meant to comfort us, somehow, but it did not.

One of the things that I can't forget from that day is seeing my baby sister Joanie wake up with a start, at the dinner table, once all the commotion began. Her face rose from the table and turned immediately dark pink as she broke into tears. I knew it was from the sudden waking, but knew, too, that what we had to tell her would lock that fresh sorrow into her little heart-shaped face. I picked Joanie up, and she clung to me, wetting me with her tears, her legs enfolding me, keeping me there on earth to watch out for her.

Uncle Frank had kept Dad's store open because he knew his brother would hate for it to be sold, but the truth was that in 1970 the last place people wanted to shop was a store called Carl's Corsets. Girls were going braless—I was—and panty hose were making the girdles my dad had built his business on obsolete. Uncle Frank was trying to modernize. He carried fishnet panty hose and paisley lounging pajamas with Nehru collars. Little did he know they were already out of style.

On the days I worked there I sat at the counter reading magazines, until I was interrupted once an hour or so by a customer. Aside from our old-lady mainstays, there were brides buying their trousseaus. The bridal line was practically our only moneymaker. Times had changed, but girls still wanted sheer vanilla negligees and pink satin mules and garters. I enjoyed helping them pick the stuff out, although it seemed otherworldly to me. I didn't think I'd ever get married.

I thought we'd do better business if we'd start carrying some wilder stuff: push-up bras, tiger-print bra-and-panty sets, even crotchless panties. But I didn't have the nerve to suggest this to Uncle Frank; he'd just say no and lecture me about keeping up Daddy's high standards. Occasionally a "sleaze catalog," as Uncle Frank called them, would arrive in our mail, and I thought seriously about forging my uncle's signature on the order form.

If my cousin Tommy were here, he'd do it in a second. I missed working with him at the store, the way he'd dash in and kiss the mannequins on their red-painted lips or line up a row of lacy garters on his biceps. Daddy used to reprimand Tommy for his antics, but I think he secretly enjoyed them.

In high school Tommy and I began to hang out together, outside of family gatherings. All my girlfriends had big crushes on him, and why not? He had champagne-blond hair and dark green eyes. He was a star basketball player and a great dancer. Knowing all I did of Tommy, I could make or break him with girls at school. That's when he started being nicer to me.

Our first big disagreement as teenagers erupted as we came close to graduating from high school. We started arguing all the time about Vietnam. Our parents did, too: my parents felt the war was a mistake; Tommy's parents thought it was the right thing to do. Tommy was drafted right out of high school, and he had no desire to resist.

Now that he had been over there for a year and a half, none of us knew what to think about the politics of the war, we just wanted him home. I participated in war protests all the time when I was at school in Austin, but I wrote to Tommy every week anyway.

The night before he left for Nam I begged him to run away. I offered to drive him up to Canada.

"Like your Malibu would make it that far," Tommy teased.

When it was clear he intended to go, I couldn't stop crying. We were down in my basement rec room alone, listening to Janis Joplin sing "A Piece of My Heart" and drinking Gallo wine.

Tommy held me in his arms and we danced a little, staggering around on the damp cement floor. Tommy kissed me and laughed at how red my tongue and lips were from the wine.

"I'll be fine," he told me.

His hair had already been shaved off, and I petted his head. It felt soft as baby's hair.

A few weeks after the day I'd banged my head in Mom's closet, toward the end of June, I saw another gecko, in the bathroom one night. He was smaller than my baby finger and transparent pink. His tail had stripes of gray and was longer than his body. When he skittered across the floor he seemed to be twitching his hips, but I suppose he had none. I got him to crawl onto a *Time* magazine, then carried him outside and tipped him off the porch onto the lawn.

I pulled a joint out of my pocket and lit it; it would help me get sleepy. I lay on the glider swing, my feet dangling into Joanie's wading pool. I pictured my dad asleep on this swing in his yellow seersucker pajamas. On hot nights he would lie out here before bedtime, to get some breeze. Often my mother and I had had to wake him for bed.

I remembered one night, when I was about sixteen, when I had found Daddy in the backyard smoking one of his congratulatory cigars from Joanie's birth six months earlier. I had gone outside to gather up the water hose, something Daddy had asked me to do in the afternoon, but which I had just remembered to do after midnight. There was Daddy, sitting cross-legged on the glider puffing on his cigar, illuminated by moonlight in his lemon pajamas.

"Shh. . . ." Daddy had whispered.

He meant, don't tell Mom about the cigar.

"You'll have to change your pj's or she'll smell it," I whispered back, nestling on the swing beside him.

After I gave the swing a terrific push, my father and I had both laughed loudly in the dark.

Now, the smell of the marijuana smoke seemed to attract fireflies. Tommy had always been a firefly magnet. At family gatherings, we'd look up from eating big bowls of butter brickle ice cream and see Tommy with a couple of fireflies lighting on him, one at his shoulder, one at his foot, gold and luminous.

The first of July, though I felt a little guilty about supporting her habit, I accepted Mom's invitation to accompany her to Dallas on a shopping expedition. We dropped Joanie off at Aunt Ruthie's early in the morning and hit the highway in my dark blue Malibu. It was the time of year when it was hot already by 8 A.M. My car had air-conditioning that worked, but just barely. The car was filled with the sweet sounds of Motown. Mom chewed her Clark clove gum, two sticks at a time, steeping the car in its spicy smell, and we talked about what we would buy from Neiman's. The sun shimmered panes of pale yellow on the highway, and tiny hair coils were springing up at Mom's temples from the humidity in spite of the A.C., and we were going to shop for *fall* clothes, according to Mom. We got to Neiman's just as the doors were being unlocked, 10 A.M.

"We are coming in at Men's Cologne, we are coming in at Men's Cologne," my mother chanted softly as we entered the store. So we'd remember later when we left. I smelled Aramis, which brought to mind one of my favorite professors, someone I hoped to seduce that fall. Aramis also made me think of Tommy— he wore it, too, and it was one of our standard Christmas presents for him. Mom suggested we put together a whole Neiman's care package to send to Tommy in Vietnam, so, in addition to the Aramis, we bought him expensive pima cotton socks and some imported handkerchiefs. Then we went to the candy department and picked out some candies that we hoped wouldn't melt.

I admit I didn't know much about Nam, but I knew enough to realize that these were perhaps not the most useful gifts we could be sending Tommy. I think my mother must have thought of this war as being a gentleman's war, much like my father's

World War II experience, which was as a weatherman, stateside. But I knew this war was different.

We had our gifts for Tommy wrapped and then moved on to the junior department. The things Mom wanted me to have seemed comical to me. She selected three black cocktail dresses, all of them tent-style, indistinguishable from each other, I thought. "One will do, Mom," I said, knowing I would likely never even wear the one.

After a while, she gave up and put some money into my hand. "You pick out some things you like, and I'll pick up some things for Joanie and me, and then we'll meet for lunch in two hours, okay?"

I proceeded to the men's department to buy a plain white cotton shirt. I sneaked into a men's dressing room. My nipples scratched against the stiff cotton. I felt slightly thrilled by being in the men's dressing room; I inhaled the cologne smells and a slight gym-sock smell. Then I heard my name being paged, telling me to come to Customer Service. Shit. Mom had probably fainted again. And I'd made her eat a big breakfast! I changed back into my sundress, dropped the shirt, and ran out of the men's room, enjoying the look of surprise on the salesman's face.

I ran for the escalator and scaled it two stairs at a time. I dashed to where I thought Customer Service was, but no; I asked a saleslady where it was, and I had to ride the escalator to the next floor up. I lunged up the last bit of moving stair and raced over to Customer Service, breathless by then. Mom was sitting there, looking tiny in an overstuffed armchair. Someone had gotten her a cup of coffee from the restaurant. She looked pale. "Mother!" I said accusingly.

"Oh, honey."

I saw she was crying. "Mom, what? Are you all right?" I took the coffee cup out of her shaking hands. "Mom?"

A saleslady materialized beside us. "Your mother got some upsetting news over the phone," the woman said.

I stared at the woman's stacked black bun and tried to make

sense of her. "Is something wrong with Joanie?" I asked. I nearly screamed it. "Mom?"

"No, honey, it's your cousin Tommy—"

"What about Tommy?" *He's not dead, he's not dead.*

"Ruthie called . . . Tommy's coming home," Mom said.

"But that's good news!" I said. I pictured Tommy vaulting through the door at the airport, back home where he belonged, letting Aunt Ruthie kiss on him, receiving a manly hug from Uncle Frank. His hair would have grown out a bit, I thought, by now from the Army buzz; it would be pale gold and spiky.

"He's hurt pretty bad, honey. He lost an arm."

I sank to the floor beside Mom. He's alive, I told myself, that's the important thing. But Tommy minus an arm . . . I thought of his arms around me when we'd danced that last night in my basement. Before I knew I was crying, a splash of tears scalded my arm.

Aunt Ruthie had called us at the store with the news because she needed us to come back and take care of Joanie. On the drive back to Annette, I tried to pay attention to the road but could think of nothing but Tommy. Mom said one day on the news she'd seen some handicapped men playing basketball in wheel-chairs.

My mother's illogic made me tear up again. I had to stop crying so I could see the road. "But Tommy can walk, Mom," I said.

When I thought of Tommy in high school I saw him holding a basketball aloft, his muscles visibly flexing as he sent the ball sailing.

Mom and I made a bunch of food and took it over to Uncle Frank and Aunt Ruthie's. Hamburger casserole, banana bread, pineapple upside-down cake. It was silly, because Tommy wasn't coming home for a week, and really we were making it for him.

Uncle Frank talked about when he was in the war, and he showed us a jagged white scar that went down his side.

83

Aunt Ruthie said her arm wouldn't stop hurting. "I think I felt when he lost it. Because the day they said it happened I was down in the basement, and I reached to get a box of canning jars, and suddenly this pain about knocked me flat. Frank told me I just pulled something, but when it happened, I thought of Tommy suddenly. Frank said it was just because Tommy loves grape jelly so, and I was fixing to put some up, but I think it was me feeling the . . ."

Nobody could say it. Explosion. Gunfire. Nothing close to it.

The news didn't mean much to Joanie yet. She played with her Barbie and Ken dolls. They wore prom clothes, and their stiff, cool plastic arms embraced awkwardly.

After serving Mom and Aunt Ruthie, Uncle Frank poured me out a Tom Collins. Suddenly I was a grown-up.

Mom and Joanie went right to bed as soon as we got home, Joanie in Mom's bed. I tucked them in, kissing my mom on her cheek and Joanie on her forehead. I went to Daddy's study, which was mostly as he'd left it, except for some stacks of Joanie's games and puzzles on top of his wooden file cabinet. I sat in Daddy's armchair and smelled the arms. I could still smell a bit of him, but I was afraid that before long the smell would leave. Licorice and ink: he figured accounts in that chair. And wrote little notes. He liked to get up before everyone in the morning and write a tiny weather prediction note, which he taped to the bathroom mirror. "Sweaters, girls!"

Mom had given some of Daddy's clothes to Uncle Frank and donated some to rummage sales, but there were still some things in the study closet. I slipped my arms into his red-and-black plaid flannel robe. It was soft and nubby at the same time. I sat in the chair hugging myself, my hands meeting under the large cuffs.

I went to bed, but I couldn't go to sleep. I tried to remember if Tommy had left a girlfriend behind in Annette. He'd had so many, but if I remembered right, he'd made a clean break before he went to boot camp.

I tiptoed downstairs and rolled a joint on top of Joanie's "The Grasshopper and the Ants" story album. The record was a hand-me-down from me. I remembered listening to it with Tommy when we were kids. He could do a dead-on imitation of the grasshopper who had sat around all summer and fall having a good, lazy time while the industrious ants harvested crumbs every day for food and built little homes out of leaves and twigs. When the cold weather came, the grasshopper had nothing. "Oh, ants, won't you help me?" I could hear Tommy's plaintive cry and then his laughter after. "Won't you *pleez?*"

After a few hits I sat on the living room floor eating Chee-tos. I saw a little gecko skittering across the floor. I tapped my foot and he stopped. If I don't move, she won't see me, he seemed to think. His pink skin was so transparent I could see the grain of the wood floor right through it. I took a tiny Chee-to and placed it on the floor close to the gecko. I pictured it as a little baton for him to carry. He turned his head slightly to look at the Chee-to, and his tail pulsed a bit.

I gently swept the gecko onto the grasshopper album, along with his baton, and took them outside to the grass. The gecko scrambled slightly as I tipped the slick cover; then I couldn't see him anymore.

It was starting to rain, a very fine mist blown sideways by the wind. I lay down on the chaise lounge on our screened-in back porch and cried myself to sleep with the rain sifting over me.

I helped Uncle Frank out at the store the next day. I drank a whole pot of coffee in the morning and paced around the store. Between remembering my dad in the back of the store with his hand flying over the adding machine and phantom images of Tommy in the store feeling up the mannequins under their nylon nighties, I spent the whole day tearing up. Then I would pull myself together to greet the rare customer that ventured into the store. My grade school math teacher came in and bought some panty girdles. At lunchtime, Mom brought Joanie in and asked me to take my sister

to lunch while she watched the store. She gave me money and
said to buy Joanie some coloring books, too. We went to Doreen's
Drugstore and ordered grilled cheese and fries and cherry Cokes.

Joanie was unusually quiet. She skated her fries around in a
puddle of ketchup for a long time. "He won't be able to play loop-
de-loop with me," she said finally.

Tommy used to let her climb his legs, and then she'd do a
flip as she held onto his arms.

"No," I said. I chewed up an ice cube. "But he can still do
this." And I twirled her seat till I saw her come back around
laughing.

Aunt Ruthie and Uncle Frank went without us to pick Tommy
up at the airport. "We don't want to wear him out; he's still
recovering," Aunt Ruthie said.

We went over later for hamburgers. In the car I noticed my
mother was wearing a new sundress; the tag hung from the halter
tie at the back. If I didn't get it off, Aunt Ruthie would torment
Mom about it. The price of Mom's dress was more than Aunt
Ruthie would spend on three sundresses. Daddy's Swiss Army
knife was in the glove compartment. I took the teeny scissors and
cut off the tag.

"Thanks!" Mom said. She squeezed my hand.

The pocketknife made me think of Daddy's fishing hat.
Tommy and Daddy were both wild for fishing. Once in a while I
would go along on their fishing trips, but I never fit in. They had
their own fishing language, fish stories. Mom planned to give
Daddy's hat to Tommy at Christmas.

Fishing was something Tommy could do with one arm,
maybe. I could bait hooks for him. I started crying. When Mom
heard me sniffling, she shot me a look.

"We have to be strong for Tommy."

Tommy was out on the porch smoking a cigarette when we
pulled up. He stood up and first I saw his scarred face; there was
a slash across his forehead, punctuating his green eyes like a check

mark. His hair, as I had pictured it, was spiking up crazily. He tugged at the corner of his lip, like he always did when he was nervous. He wore jeans and a white T-shirt. The tee was blinding white against his tanned skin. The left sleeve was folded up neatly and pinned.

Joanie ran up the porch steps, then paused.

"Sugar bun!" Tommy growled softly. He sat on the porch swing and patted his leg; she climbed onto his knee and kissed his cheek. They swung on the porch swing a few seconds.

Then I fell against him, hugging him, smelling his Clorox and Aramis and cigarette smell. I kissed him on the lips and he tasted like Jack Daniel's. There was a tumbler full of it on the porch floor. "Roxie!" he whispered.

"Roxanne, let me at him," my mom said. I stepped back and let Mom hug and kiss on Tommy.

Joanie reached over and was the first of us to touch it. She petted at the fold of his T-shirt. "Does it hurt?"

"Not so much anymore, sugar," Tommy told her. "Not with your magic touch."

We walked around the house to the back porch and watched Uncle Frank cook the burgers. I sat on the back stoop with Tommy, holding his hand.

"You look like boyfriend and girlfriend, for land sakes, not cousins." Aunt Ruthie laughed a little high-pitched squeak, then frowned at us a bit.

When Uncle Frank went into the house to freshen our drinks, Tommy went over to flip the burgers. He made a show of flipping them with one hand, but one flipped onto the grass. Aunt Ruthie's chow dog, Mitzi, raced over and grabbed the half-grilled patty. She dropped it and picked it up a few times till it was cool, then inhaled it.

"You know I always make a bunch of extra hamburgers, Tommy, don't worry," Aunt Ruthie said. "Mitzi, you pig!" She swatted Mitzi with a dish towel.

*   *   *

Tommy was quiet during dinner. He carefully squirted ketchup onto his hamburger. We tried not to watch, but we were all drawn to his every move.

He went out to the pantry to make himself another drink. Aunt Ruthie's eyebrow shot up. "He's drinking too much," she said to Uncle Frank.

Aunt Ruthie got up and stacked a high pile of dirty plates; forks and knives stuck out wildly. I followed her out of the dining room, picking up a trail of silver as I went. Aunt Ruthie stood at the stove stirring hot fudge sauce, the kind that hardens as it hits the ice cream. She wiped at her eyes with a tea towel.

In the pantry I found Tommy sitting on a footstool staring into his glass of bourbon. "Hot fudge!" I said, before bursting into tears.

He held me to him. "Hot fudge, Roxanne," Tommy said. "The only chocolate I got over there was turning white and usually had bugs. Mom's hot fudge . . ." He wiped my face dry with his T-shirt.

Back in the dining room, he ate three bowls of ice cream and sauce. "This is the best thing I ever ate."

A couple of days later Tommy came into the store to hang out with me. He paced around a lot and went out back to smoke a cigarette every few minutes. I finally got him to hold still when I showed him one of the sleazy lingerie catalogs I had hidden under the counter. He circled his favorites, little maid outfits and panties with crotches made of feathers.

"Let's order 'em!" he said.

"Your dad would kill us."

Once when I was marking some panty hose packets, I felt Tommy's hand on my hair.

"I missed this hair."

I held very still and let him pet it for a long time. Then the bell at the door clattered noisily as a pair of old ladies came inside. Tommy darted to the rear of the store to smoke again.

Whenever anyone came into the store, Tommy shrank to the back. A couple of his high school friends, Monica and Julie, came in, and I couldn't decide what to say to them. Monica spied him in the back.

"Is that Tommy back there?" Monica cried.

He waved his arm, but stayed in the back.

"Tommy, come out here!" Monica said.

"Tommy!" her friend Julie echoed.

He emerged, holding his left shoulder back like they might not notice.

"Tommy," Monica said, "you made it back from Nam!" She hugged him like there was nothing at all wrong. Then I remembered. Monica had lost her brother in Vietnam. An arm gone must have seemed like just a little scratch, to her.

Julie hung back, stammering something about how they had to hurry. She snatched a pair of hose off the stack I'd been pricing and thrust some money at me. "Good to see you, Tommy," she said. And she began backing out of the place, dragging Monica with her.

"Julie!" Monica said. "What is *wrong* with you?"

"I gotta go, too," Tommy said. He smiled and moved back toward the stockroom.

By the afternoon Tommy started horsing around a little like he used to. He tried on a purple negligee.

"Nothing up my sleeve," he said, in a Bullwinkle-cartoon voice.

He dangled the transparent sleeve before my eyes. Later he found an armless mannequin in the back room.

"Hey, I think I've found the girl for me," he said. He began to soft-shoe around the store, holding her.

As the summer wore on, I considered skipping the fall semester at school. I felt like Tommy needed me. He told me to go on back, but every time I looked at my suitcase I felt my stomach twist.

89

The middle of August, a few days before I was set to return to Austin, Uncle Frank, Aunt Ruthie, and Mom took Joanie to a double feature at the drive-in. My aunt had asked me to fix Tommy some dinner; I made a Jeno's packaged pizza. After we drank a couple of beers, I rolled out the pizza dough on the counter and started giggling when it stuck there. After I pried it up with a spatula, Tommy tossed the round of pizza dough in the air and caught it. He tossed it again and caught it. I had to make him stop because the dough had turned see-through. When we ate the pizza later, sauce dripped through the holes.

After we ate, we went outside and Tommy lit some leftover sparklers from the Fourth of July. I watched the swoop of his arm as the sparklers sizzled through the night. The singed scent lingered while we ate ice-cream drumsticks on the tree swing. I put an Aretha Franklin record on in the living room and cranked the volume up as far as I could without the neighbors yelling.

"Gonna find me an angel, to fly away with me," Aretha sang.

"I used to be such a good dancer," Tommy said.

"I bet you still are," I said. I dropped my empty paper cone on the lawn and so did Tommy. "Come on."

"I can't hold you," Tommy said.

"Let me hold you," I told him.

And he did. We rocked back and forth for a long time, till we heard the record needle softly thumping over and over again. Tommy kissed me. We fell to the grass, and we kissed for a long time.

"Go ahead," I told him.

He untied the string of my peasant blouse and put his hand on my left breast. Then on the other.

"I can't hold two at once," he murmured. He was laughing softly, and crying.

"It's okay. I feel it more when it's one at a time, anyway." I realized this was true.

He let me take off his shirt. The stub was but a slight rise beneath his skin; the skin was surprisingly smooth, glossy even. I kissed it all over. I could feel Tommy's sharp intake of breath at first, then his regular breath beneath me. He felt me with his strong large-boned fingers.

"That hand," I told him. "It's got . . . extra powers."

I saw my last gecko of the summer before I went back to school. I was washing dishes and looked up to the kitchen window and saw him hanging from the screen. I could see a dark heart or two pulsing beneath his thin pink skin. His toes were curled around the tiny black wires of the screen. He was hanging on.

Wedding Boots

"ROXANNE, HONEY, YOU WON'T BELIEVE THIS," MY AUNT RUTHIE WHISPERED NOISILY ACROSS SEVERAL hundred miles of long-distance wire.

Her phone conversations nearly always started out this way. I set my Coke down on a nearby bookshelf and prepared to be shocked. To my surprise, I actually was.

"Your mother is *dating!*"

I'd have believed "Your mother flew to Venus" a little quicker. True, my father had been dead for nearly eight years. And my mother, at fifty-two, was still young. But Mom dating? An image flittered through my head. Mom at Doreen's Drugstore sharing a banana split with *some man.* From there I careened over to Mom at the bar on the edge of town, Bisbee's, drinking a martini with *some man.* My mother's lips carefully lipsticked in cherry red nibbling an olive off of a swizzle stick. Lord.

"I don't believe it," I said.

"Roxpie, it's the dead truth. There's a new fellow in town named Dirk Bixby. Can you imagine? Dirk, what kind of name is that?" my aunt asked.

"I . . ."

"So anyhow, while your Uncle Frank's been laid up with that misery in his back, your mom's been managing the store. Not doing so bad, Frank says, though she orders a little high. So this character, this *Dirk* moves to town and he comes into the store and asks your mother if she sells . . . well, you know, naughty panties and such at the store. Turns out he's an *entrepreneur*, he calls himself." I heard my aunt sigh in exasperation. "One of his little businesses is a line of these naughty things; Roxanne, your daddy would turn over in his grave. But this man, after your mother says no to ordering this, this *stuff*, he shows up at church the next Sunday. Imagine that! And asks her to go to lunch after! Joanie had this youth group outing, so your mother went to lunch with him. They went out to that little barbecue place out by the city limits, that place that serves beer on Sundays, and Dirk had two bottles. On a Sunday! Your mother said they had barbecue sandwiches and a delicious raisin pie for dessert."

I sat down and pulled a cigarette out of my purse and lit it. "Hmm," I said. There was no rushing a story of my aunt's.

I heard my uncle calling Ruthie in the background.

"Rox, honey, I've gotta go. Your uncle needs me."

"But Ruthie! How did we get from raisin pie to dating?"

"Sorry, honey. Bye bye."

Luckily I was heading to Annette the next day for the Fourth of July weekend to plan my wedding with Mom, so I would get the scoop on Dirk then. I told myself Aunt Ruthie was probably just exaggerating. Mom would have told me if she were dating, wouldn't she? And what was so wrong with Mom dating? I asked myself. Did I want my mother to be alone the rest of her life?

After all, I would be marrying Fritz Beacon over Christmas. I was so happy, I wanted all the world to be coupled up. But as good as I felt about my impending marriage, my stomach fluttered when I thought about the wedding itself. I wasn't good with all those details, and I was afraid Mom and Ruthie would railroad me into a ruffly gown or derail the chocolate cake I had planned for the reception. Fritz had wisely chosen to steer clear of this wedding meeting. He was toiling over his dissertation on jazz theory and had ears only for Dizzy Gillespie, not for the wedding march.

"When you get there, call me." Fritz had been checking all my car's levels and his hands were streaked with dark, shimmering fluids. He held his hands behind him like a kid hiding something from his teacher and kissed me passionately. "Huh," he said. "It's hard to kiss without your hands."

I drove off with my tape deck blaring Willie Nelson and looked behind me in my rearview mirror to see Fritz, arms still akimbo, grinning blindly into the July sun.

I had met Fritz at the library when I was a work-study student. At the time, I was new at my job, and into being officious, which I thought was a compulsory trait for librarians. I came upon Fritz in one of the back carrels; he was wearing earphones and listening, I later found out, to jazz. He was eating what was clearly a very ripe pear, and was dribbling juice all over his chin, the carrel, and his torn blue jeans, too.

"Sir, you can't eat in here."

I had gotten into the habit of calling men "sir" at the coffee shop where I'd worked previously, and though I knew it was absurd to call fellow students "sir," I couldn't break myself of the habit.

"Ma'am, I cannot?" Fritz replied in a low and serious voice. Only his pivoting eyebrows betrayed him.

"Nuh . . . uh," I said. I tried not to smile. I had already taken in his zany red hair and freckled, muscular forearms. He was wearing a burgundy T-shirt that made his skin pale as cream.

Fritz proffered his pear. "Hungry?" he asked me.

"Nah, I never share food until at least the second date," I said. Just then *Jane Eyre* slid off a stack I was carrying and crushed my little toe. "Youch!" I said, a bit too loudly for a library.

Fritz reached down to touch my tennis shoe and asked if I was okay. He asked if my toe was too badly hurt to dance with him, then asked me to go to a party with him that Friday. The rest was . . . well, the rest had been the last two years of my life.

When I drove into Annette it was almost dinnertime. I pulled up to our house and savored the pale blue paint on the shutters.

My daddy had painted them the summer before he died, and I knew they would never be repainted.

When I walked through the door, my eleven-year-old sister, Joanie, immediately began to complain to me about Mom not buying her a princess phone for her room till Christmas. "How am I supposed to wait till then?" she screeched.

"Can't I have a hug first?" I asked her. When I hugged her I saw her hair was down to her waist. The way it swung out behind made it seem like a separate entity altogether.

"Roxanne!" Mom called from the kitchen. I entered the kitchen and saw her hoisting a tray of biscuits from the oven. "Hi, honey. Are you hungry?"

When I hugged her I drank in her smells: gardenia perfume, face powder, and Aqua Net hair spray.

"I'm hungry."

"Tomorrow we'll have barbecue with Ruthie and Frank . . . and did I tell you Tommy's bringing his girlfriend?"

"Minnie? Is that her name? Fritz is sorry he couldn't make it. He had a meeting with his dissertation chair tonight, and tomorrow he's spending the day in the library. He wants to get his defense out of the way before the wedding."

"Well, we'll miss him. When he was here Memorial Day weekend, Frank told me they had a great 'man-to-man' talk. Frank thinks he's swell."

"He *is* swell." I smiled. Uncle Frank's opinion meant a lot to me. He was so much like his brother, my dear, departed daddy.

"By the way, Frank is barbecuing practically a whole side of beef this weekend," Mom told me. She handed me a glass of white wine, poured herself one, then went back to her dinnertime tasks.

"Will Dirk be joining us?"

My mother dropped a carrot peeling on her foot and stared at me in surprise. "That blabbermouth Ruthie!"

Joanie came in the room then and Mom mouthed, "Later," to me.

We ate meatloaf and mashed potatoes and brown-sugar car-

95

rots, and for dessert, lemon pudding cake. Back in Austin I was
on a diet, but it never paid to try that at my mother's house.

Mom and I lingered over coffee, while Joanie went over to
her friend's house to listen to records.

"Joanie doesn't know I'm dating," Mom said.

"How can she not know?" I asked. I licked lemon cream off
the tines of my fork.

"She's pretty oblivious. You were that way when you were
eleven, too. All she thinks about is that telephone."

"Are you afraid she won't like him? What's he like?"

"I'm sort of afraid, I guess. She remembers Daddy better than
you think."

"Yeah. I know. So what's this guy like?"

"Well . . ." Mom began to curlicue a strand of hair around her
finger. "I guess Aunt Ruthie's already given you an earful. She
doesn't approve, because he handles a more risqué line of mer-
chandise. But he has a lot of other irons in the fire, too. He's a
nice man, Roxanne. And he's crazy about me."

Mom pulled a sweetheart necklace out of her blouse and
showed me. "I know I'm too old for this," Mom said. "He's not
coming to the barbecue. I just don't think Ruthie and Frank are
ready to deal with it all. Neither am I, for that matter. We've only
been out at night twice, nights when Joanie was at slumber parties.
Both times, we went to movies at the Plymouth."

"And then?" Did I really want to know, I wondered?

"And then we went to Jerry's Dairy King, for milk shakes. It's
very strange dating when you're in your fifties. I don't know what
to do with myself; I'm like a teenager."

"But no pimples," I teased. I thought if I joked around about
the whole thing, I would feel okay about it. But no.

The next morning Mom woke me at 7, and we drank coffee
and ate hot-from-the-oven blueberry muffins out on the glider
swing in the backyard. I was worried I'd have to buy bigger jeans
before I left town that weekend. It was still a bit cool at this hour;

Mom's vines of beefeater tomatoes still had a mist of dew on them, and her impatiens were the color of rabbit ears. As much as I told myself I wasn't a small-town girl anymore—and I swore it up and down when I was in Austin—in many ways I still was. Austin had live music, art, festivals, always something to do. I thought I was more suited to Austin, but when I was home in Annette, I doubted myself. When I was a teenager it made me grumpy that around every street corner there was someone I knew, but now, coming home I realized how much I enjoyed it. When I'd gone to get half-and-half for our coffee last night at the Minimax I'd run into a good four or five people I knew during my ten-minute errand. It was a great feeling.

Mom said, "Don't you love the morning before it gets hot?"

"Yes," I said, "all twenty minutes or so!" This was shaping up to be a really hot summer; I wasn't exaggerating.

"So, let's talk about your wedding," Mom said. She smoothed her bright-flowered, cotton housedress beneath the plate of muffins. "I want your wedding to be what you want it to be. However big or small, however plain or fancy," Mom told me.

"I believe you," I told her. "Let's just keep Aunt Ruthie out of it!"

"Honey, you know we can't. Sure, Tommy will probably get married sometime, but it's not the same planning from the groom's side. She wants so much to be a part of this, honey, and she loves you so."

"I know it." I sipped coffee and fought off the urge to lick muffin crumbs off my plate. "I love her, too; you know I do, but she makes me a little nuts."

Right on cue, Ruthie showed up yoo-hooing from the back door. She'd poured herself a cup of coffee and was carrying a plate of cinnamon rolls. I unbuttoned the waist of my jeans and had one. Ruthie had brought some bridal magazines. We thumbed through all of them, but I couldn't imagine myself in any of the gowns. All those froufrous, illusion necklines, flounces, and veils, they weren't for me. I wanted a simple dress in ice blue, not white. And a rose in my hair; that was it. I pictured Fritz in his Mexican muslin shirt with a bolo tie and a winsome smile. Most of all, I desired a small, intimate wedding with our best friends and family. We'd eat homemade cake and drink champagne and dance to Marvin Gaye and Smokey Robinson.

Ruthie held forth on sweetheart necklines and tacky head-dresses. Mom and I said little. Finally, Aunt Ruthie asked to look at my engagement ring. I held it up to her and she seemed mystified. It was an antique garnet ring I loved dearly, but Ruthie said an engagement ring wasn't an engagement ring without a diamond.

That night at the barbecue I got to meet Tommy's latest squeeze, who was not named Minnie after all: her name was Kitty. Tommy seemed calmed and happy. The last time I had seen him, a year before this, he had shown up at my apartment in Austin one night at three in the morning, strung out on drugs and ranting about some girl who'd left him. He'd cried, then he'd eaten up a bowl of hard candy that was on my bookshelf, and had fallen asleep on my lap.

Tommy had alternated between drinking too much and doing too many drugs for all the years since he'd come back from Vietnam. I guessed we could be grateful that at least he took turns on his extremes. I didn't know what to do for him but to listen to him. He told me stories of things he had seen and done in Vietnam, and it wasn't hard for me to understand his addictions, after hearing these. His stories gave me nightmares, and I had only heard them, not been shattered by them, as Tommy had. Healing takes as long as it takes, I figured.

Now he was back in college and at long last had decided to major in botany. I had gotten a degree in library science, and Kitty was working on a degree in theater, so the three of us had a little trouble finding a common link. I could see Tommy enjoyed Kitty's theatricality, but I found it just plain silly.

Tommy was sitting on a lawn chair holding his ancient dog, Mitzi. He worked her ears, kneading the floppy bits between his fingers tenderly. If Kitty had not been in love with Tommy before now, I guessed that seeing this side of Tommy would nail it. But I soon saw she was already in love. At the very least, she knew he liked plenty of lime with his gin and tonics.

"Hey, Rox-bunny, remember the time you tried to eat a lime?" Tommy turned to Kitty. "She shook about six packets of sugar over it first. Cheating, absolute cheating."

"Ha!" I cried. "Three packets. And it still turned my tongue inside out."

"Roxie, when you get married can I be the flower boy?" Tommy began giggling.

"Tommy, you'd be the ring bearer," Kitty told him.

"Do not take him seriously!" I advised.

Kitty blushed, then she sipped at her drink.

"Sorry, Tommy, this is like an old-fashioned hippie wedding," I said. "I'll walk up on my own with no procession before or foofaraw after."

Tommy frowned. "Does my mom know?"

"She's been informed but is not getting it. You know how she is . . ."

"Say no more," Tommy said, waving his hand in the air. Mitzi shifted and moaned luxuriously.

Uncle Frank walked by waving a large plate of ribs at us suggestively. But we were already full of meat and just waiting for a dessert or two.

"I love weddings," Kitty offered. "What kind of music will you have?"

"Well, I'm in favor of a lot of Motown. That's for the dancing. And Fritz will want some jazz; that's his baby."

"I'd want show tunes," Kitty said.

Tommy looked apprehensive.

I thought it best to change the subject. "So, Tommy, have you met this guy Mom's going out with?"

"No, I haven't," Tommy said. "But I've heard a thing or two. And I'm on his side. The store needs a few wench's outfits and feather-crotched panties."

At first I laughed, but then I got a bit panicky. Was this guy dating Mom just to try to get his scanty stuff into the store? That smooth-talking swindler, he was just using Mom! Just then Mom walked over, bringing bowls full of peach cobbler with mounds of vanilla ice cream melting onto them.

With my mouth full of warm cinnamony cobbler and cool vanilla, it was easy to forget my worries for the time being.

The next morning I knocked for a second on Joanie's door and then walked in with a load of her clothes fresh from the dryer. I came in on Joanie playing with a Barbie doll. When she saw me, she dropped Barbie like her hair was on fire, and told me she'd been cleaning stuff out from under her bed and had found "that old thing."

I told her I'd played with my Barbies till I was thirteen, which was true, but she accused me of making it up. I left out the part where my friend Penny had ridiculed me for it.

Whenever I came home, Joanie liked me to play with her hair. Mom was all thumbs with rollers, so Joanie had almost a physical craving for hair fooling. First, I brushed out the expanse of molasses brown hair, and it was as slippery as could be, falling over my hands all mermaidy wavy. She didn't need hair rollers one bit, but I told her how my old baby-sitter, Bitsy Monroe, used to roll her hair on juice cans, and then nothing would do but that I roll Joanie's on cans. We went down to the kitchen and rooted around and found a few clean ones, and then we made up a pitcher of lemonade and a bottle of orange juice and washed out the cans.

We put on our bathing suits and went out to the back swing. I wetted Joanie's hair down with water and Dippity-Do, and rolled her hair onto the cans and clipped them together with clothespins. After that we spread a big quilt on the grass and squirted each other with creamy globs of Coppertone. We lay on the quilt squinting into the sun; Joanie periodically whined about the cans hurting her neck. I glanced over and noticed my baby sister was starting to grow breasts, little niblets beneath her red and white checked top. The suit was a hand-me-down from me which she'd never be caught dead in at the pool, but it was fine for tanning. I felt myself drifting off to sleep; some cool shade started to envelope me, and when I opened my eyes, there was Mom.

"Hi, honey!" she said. She was up fresh from her nap and had had her afternoon coffee, I gathered from her perkiness. "Honey, I hate to bother you, but you said you'd help me can some peaches today, and since you're going back tomorrow . . ."

"Okay."

Joanie was out like a light, and we worried she'd sunburn. "Is that the phone I hear?" my mom shouted liltingly, and Joanie popped up like a jack-in-the-box. She was dashing to the house when Mom said, "Or maybe not. . . ."

Joanie glowered at us, then stormed inside to take a shower.

"Very tricky!" I complimented my mom.

After we had blanched and peeled a hundred peaches or so, I noticed a tear trickling down Mom's cheek. At first I thought it was perspiration from the peach steam, but no. When I asked her what was wrong, Mom told me that Aunt Ruthie had called to say that she and Frank wanted to chip in on paying for my wedding. Clearly, she'd told Mom, I was asking for a simple wedding, and a simple dress, because I feared Mom couldn't afford to pay for better.

"Ooooh!" I shouted. "She makes me so mad! She thinks she knows everything!"

My mom had little bits of peach peel all up and down her arms and they glistened in the sunlight. "Honey, we can get you a dress from Neiman's if you want, and we can afford a really good baker and get a band for the reception. Your dad invested very wisely, and . . ."

"Mom, Mom! No! I don't want a fancy fluffed-up dress and a

veil. It's not for me; I'm not the type! And I don't want a fancy white cake with swans on it or a band. It has nothing to do with money; it's just what I want, a simple wedding with friends and family. Mom, you didn't fall for Ruthie's buttinsky routine, did you?"

"Uh, no!" Mom sidled over and kissed me with her sticky arms held behind her back, reminding me of Fritz the last way I saw him. "Ruthie doesn't get to me anymore."

"Not much!" I laughed.

"Go get me the box of canning jars from the basement, honey. It's behind the water heater, under a box of—"

"I'll find them," I said.

Down in the basement in the cool darkness, I suddenly remembered the dream I had had the night before. It was my wedding day and I was wearing a stiff white dress with a long veil falling to my feet, and this was irksome enough (though Aunt Ruthie was grinning in the front row of the church... wait, a church?) and then I saw that sitting with my mother was a man, a man who must have been Dirk Bixby! He had on an orange tie, and what was that sticking out of his kerchief pocket? Fire-engine red crotchless panties! He was holding my mother's hand. And out of the back of the church, there came my father, looking as if he had just had a refreshing nap, and was not back from the dead at all. He came to the front of the church, saying, "Honey, you forgot to let me walk you up here!" and I was worried he'd see Dirk, so I tried to move forward to stop my dad, but that infernal veil had twisted at my ankles, and my teetery heels pitched me forward, and ... then I guess I woke up.

"God!" I exclaimed, my head in a box of canning jars.

"Is it a mouse?" my mother cried down the stairs.

"No, just dust," I told her.

My mom was waiting for me in the kitchen with her hair tied up in a little kerchief, looking like a wholesome housewife, not some girl-toy for a perverted, smutty panty salesman. Jesus. I was overcome with the smell of peaches, cloves, and sugar. Mom gestured at me with a big ladle, saying, "Can you wash the jars out fast, honey; we're boiling over here!"

Her face was dewy and frantic.

Later, while we were latching the lids over the peaches, Mom said, "If you want, I'll sew the blue dress for you. I've never sewn silk before, but I think I could do it."

I teared up. "Will Dirk be coming to the wedding?"

My mom looked at me and saw my damp eyes. "Honey, I don't know if we'll be seeing each other by then. It's just a bit of dating, honey, nothing serious."

"I can't believe this bothers me so much. It's not like Daddy died last week or something. I'm just worried Dirk's up to no good. He just wants you to sell that naughty underwear at Daddy's store!"

"Naughty underwear! Lord, you sound like Ruthie!"

A frightening prospect.

"Honey, you all must think I'm such a ninny! I have no intention of carrying Dirk's line at the store. That's how we met, but it has nothing to do with our dating. He knows Daddy's store is an old-fashioned store and he's not trying to hoodwink me into anything. Honey, he goes to our church! He sells other things, too; he sells carnival toys, and combs like you see in vending machines, and green-striped mints to restaurants, and lots of knick-knacks and thingamabobs. He's a salesman, that's all! The sexy lingerie is just one of his lines."

I dabbed at my cheeks with a peach-redolent rag. "Oh," was all I could say.

"You know, that blabbermouth Ruthie, she acts like she is the queen of high moral standards, but if you knew . . . once Ruthie almost left Frank for a man named Fuzz Foster!"

"What? Who the heck is Fuzz Foster?"

My mother settled back into her chair for a long story. "He taught ballroom dancing. He was what we used to call a dream-boat, in my day. Slender. He could wear those double-breasted jackets your father, bless his soul, never could. He was tall, but not too tall. A good height for dancing."

"Why did he go by Fuzz?"

"He had a crewcut and it was said to be soft as dandelion fuzz. Some ladies couldn't keep their hands off it."

"Aunt Ruthie?"

"Her, too. Of course Ruthie would never have signed up for ballroom dancing, but she won a set of lessons at a church raffle. She had always felt that the dancing at their wedding was not up to snuff, and she planned to rope Frank into a second wedding. Renewal of their vows. This didn't account for Frank getting any better at dancing, but you know how show-offy Ruthie is; she thought she could carry the day."

"Was this before Tommy was born?"

"No, after he started kindergarten. You know, in those days when women were home, it was a big deal when your only child hit kindergarten. You were at a loss. I felt that way when you went to kindergarten, too. I started knitting and crocheting all the time."

I went to the stove to put on a pot of coffee.

Mom continued: "So Ruthie would get dressed to the nines for every lesson. And wear a great deal of Shalimar. I know, because she would come for coffee sometimes afterwards, and it was like she'd been steeped in it. The Shalimar. After the third lesson, I said, 'You have a crush on Mr. Foster.' She turned red, and denied it. 'Crushes are for schoolchildren, Christina. I'm a married woman!' But I knew it was true."

"But how did she come to run *off* with him?"

"Frank and Ruthie had had this huge fight the week before Thanksgiving. You won't believe what it was about."

I wondered.

"Pecans. Frank wanted her to put pecans in the stuffing."

"Aunt Ruthie hates pecans."

"Right. She wouldn't do it. Wouldn't even consider it. Like it was morally wrong. Frank took it the wrong way, because his mother used to put in pecans. Well, you know how Ruthie gets.

She began to do spiteful things around the house. Like 'forget' half-and-half for Frank's coffee, buy the wrong color shoelaces for his dress shoes. The day before Thanksgiving, Ruthie deliberately 'forgot' to take the turkey out to thaw. Thanksgiving morning Frank went to the kitchen, and there in the kitchen sink was a big blue turkey hard as a boulder. Ruthie was gone, and Tommy was in his Hopalong Cassidy pj's eating raisin toast and watching cartoons."

I poured us some coffee.

"Thanks, hon. Anyway, Frank called me, thinking Ruthie was probably over at our house, like borrowing baked ham or something to serve, but no."

"No?"

"She was scooting down the highway in Fuzz Foster's Mustang. She had packed a little cosmetic case with a nightie and a pantsuit and, well, her diaphragm!"

I was speechless.

"Only they were just going to a dance exhibition. They stopped at a motel . . . to rest, Fuzz said. Ruthie went into the bathroom to put on her nightie. She told me she stayed in there near an hour wrestling with her conscience. While she was in there she cleaned the bathroom top to bottom, though of course it had already been clean."

"Ha!"

"Ruthie put her dress back on and came out and found Fuzz sound asleep with the blanket clutched in his hand like a five-year-old. She went to the side of the bed and put her hand on his hair and petted it for a few seconds. That's what she would allow herself. When Fuzz opened his eyes, Ruthie said, 'I can't do it, Fuzz.' 'Do what?' Fuzz asked. Ruthie knew then it really *was* just a rest stop. Evidently even on a short drive out of town, Fuzz had to stop and rest before an exhibition. They went to the coffee shop and had cherry pie and coffee and then drove on to Dallas. Ruthie felt she had to honor the commitment to dance with Fuzz. I guess it was her fifteen minutes."

"Fifteen minutes?" I asked.

"Of fame. Even though it was a holiday, a lot of people attended the exhibition. For years Ruthie was scared someone from Annette would have seen her dancing in Dallas, but no one had, or they never told Frank anyhow. Ruthie called Frank from the dance hall and told him she would be home by dark and that they would have Thanksgiving the next day, complete with pecan stuffing. It's the closest Ruthie ever came to apologizing."

"Mom, how do you know all this?"

"The night before Tommy's high school prom, do you remember? We were over at their house for dinner. Shish-kebabs?"

My mother could remember every meal eaten over time.

"Remember after dinner Ruthie was showing Tommy some steps, like the fox-trot?"

Did I. It was one of my favorite memories of Tommy. Even though he and his date would be dancing to "Stoned Soul Picnic" and the like the next night, Tommy humored his mom and let her show him these steps. But when Aunt Ruthie tried to show Tommy how to dip a girl, she burst into tears. We didn't think much of it at the time. Aunt Ruthie was going through the change and was prone to crying at the drop of a hat.

"You and Tommy went to a movie, and Daddy and Frank went to the Rotary Club. Ruthie and I stayed behind at the house and drank gin fizzes while Joanie slept on the divan. I never saw Ruthie drink so much: three or four drinks at least! She spilled the beans about the whole thing."

"And Uncle Frank never found out?"

"Frank never knew; still doesn't to this day, I imagine. She told him she had taken a bus to Dallas, seen a picture show, and then turned around and took a bus back. It made no sense, but Frank believed it anyway. He was grateful for the late Thanksgiving. Remember, we went? Had our ham on Thanksgiving and their turkey the next day. I gained five pounds!"

"I do remember. Double Thanksgiving. Of course I didn't know why." I got up and cleared our coffee cups, and Mom put jars of peaches into the cabinet, and a couple into a bag for me to take back to Austin. "I'm glad you told me that story. Now I know: Aunt Ruthie's human, after all! Who'd have guessed it?"

"Yeah, you know Ruthie and I got a lot closer after that gin fizz night. I felt just like you, that Ruthie had been lording stuff over me for years, acting like she did everything just so, and then after I knew about Fuzz, well, it gave me a softer spot in my heart for Ruthie. We've never talked about it again, though. And, Rox-anne! Don't you dare let Ruthie know I told you about this." Mom came over and grabbed my shoulders gently. "Promise?" she pleaded.

"I promise!"

Mom kissed my forehead like I was a five-year-old. "Okay then."

107

In August I got a late-night phone call from Ruthie. I pictured my aunt in a pink nylon nightie, her hair in sponge rollers, whispering into the phone so she wouldn't wake up Uncle Frank. What she whispered was this: "Rox, honey, your mom would never tell you, but she's devastated you aren't having the wedding in Annette."

For a moment my throat clenched up. Was Mom? But then I heard a nervous little hum coming over the line. Aunt Ruthie was humming, "Shine on, harvest moon." She was a nervous hum-mer when lying.

"Aunt Ruthie?"

"Yes, honey?" Hmm hmm, hmm hmm hmm. . . .

"I love you to pieces, but I don't believe you. I've talked to Mom. She's fine with the wedding in Austin. She's fine with all the stuff I've picked for the wedding."

"Rox honey . . ." She faded out, then hummed a bit.

"I'm not having a traditional wedding. And Tommy probably won't either, if he ever gets married." I sensed the humming could turn to tears, so I changed my tune. "*When* he gets married. But, Aunt Ruthie, I'll still be married. I'll still wear a pretty dress and have flowers, and we'll have a cake and wear rings and have music.

We'll still love having you at our wedding. And . . . it is *our* wedding."

I heard applause, and turned to see Fritz, sporting only glasses, white crew socks, and a large grin, clapping his hands for me.

"Okay, then, honey," Aunt Ruthie sighed. "Okay, then."

"Aunt Ruthie?"

"Yes, honey?"

"You might even have a good time."

I hung up to her soft and tender laughter.

My wedding was on the day after Christmas. We had planned an outdoor wedding, because Austin is typically warm and sunny around the holidays, but on Christmas a cold front came through, and we woke up the next morning with snowflakes swirling outside. It was my daddy's way of attending the wedding, I know it. Daddy loved snow; he had been stationed in Utah for a time during the war, and couldn't get enough of the snow. Now Daddy was raining snow down on us, tender soft flakes that shimmied through the sky and fell and frosted the grass with white.

Everyone wanted to know, what was the alternate plan? There was none. I was a bride at Zilker Park with thick white tights on under my pale blue silk, L.L. Bean boots on my feet, and my grammy's fine periwinkle wool shawl tied around my shoulders. I wore a white silk opera scarf as a hair band, to cover my cold ears. The opera scarf was a present from Dirk, from one of his many lines, and, boy, was I grateful. Fritz wore long underwear under his Mexican wedding shirt, and the guests, bundled up, stamped their feet while we said our vows. Aunt Ruthie had been appalled at the lack of an alternate plan, but stopped her grumbling when Uncle Frank hugged her hard from behind, as the wedding unfurled before her. Mom held hands with Dirk, and it was okay by me. We had met him at Thanksgiving, and I liked him in spite of myself. Joanie was coming around, too, slowly but surely. It didn't hurt that Dirk had given her an extension cord for her new princess phone for Christmas. Twenty feet of pale pink curlicued cord long enough for her to step out onto the roof outside her bedroom window and chat.

Fritz's hair glittering with snow was a sight to behold, red and sparkly and optimistic. I was so excited I bit his lip just a smidge when we kissed after the "I do's." Tommy set off a firecracker just after the kiss, and I shook my fist at him and smiled. Then the guests all flew to their cars and we drove to the reception, which was indoors, at my rich friend Susan's house, down in their rumpus room.

We had a white cake to make Ruthie happy, and there in the creamy sweep of frosting was a miniature couple, the groom red-haired, the bride brown-haired, looking for all the world like Fritz and Roxanne in a mountain of snow, in Texas.

Hospitable

FRITZ AND I DROVE INTO ANNETTE AS THE SUN ROSE OVER *THE PRETTIEST TOWN IN TEXAS* SIGN AT THE EDGE OF town. A pinkish hue glinted on the curlicued letters of the sign. Driving into downtown, we passed a few vintage cars parked by the town square. I closed my eyes and saw my daddy getting out of one. It was green, the color of a party mint, the car we'd had when I was ten. Daddy wore a striped vest Mom and I had given him for Father's Day. He looked dapper and had hair. When I finally opened my eyes we were at Mom's house.

She had called me late the night before to tell me she had to have all her "female parts" taken out, but that I didn't need to come up, she'd be fine. Fritz and I were on the highway an hour later.

Now it was 6 A.M. Mom was up. She couldn't have coffee or water or anything because of the surgery, and she didn't know what to do with herself.

"I can't read the newspaper without coffee!"

"I know, Mom." I hugged and kissed her.

I went to my sister Joanie's room to wake her up. Her hair was matted and smelled like cigarette smoke. "Joanie, baby."

She turned over and said, "What in the hell?"

"Mom didn't tell you we were coming?"

"What for?"

"The surgery! She just called me last night. Why didn't you make her call me before?"

Joanie yawned and stretched her arms. For a minute she looked five again, instead of sixteen. "Christ, the surgery is *today?*"

I fought off the urge to smack her, not for the first time in my life. "Get off your butt and throw yourself in the shower. Fast."

"Did Fritz come?"

I grabbed her arm and pulled her out of the bed. "Yep. But he has to go right back. I'll be staying a few days to help Mom out."

"Why didn't you bring me up some coffee?" Joanie said.

I made a punching gesture, one we used constantly when she was little. "Shower!"

Fritz drove us all to the hospital. Aunt Ruthie joined us there. We had to wait outside while they got Mom in her dotted patient gown and gave her some "woozy medicine," as she called it. When we went back in and stood beside her, she was giggling softly. Mom always joked that she was a cheap drunk. She looked very pale against the white sheets and thin, too—had she lost weight? I petted Mom's hair back; the little wisps at the temple made me want to cry.

Joanie held Mom's hand and said, "Everything will be okay." Mostly to herself, I think.

Fritz said, "When I come back on Sunday for Roxanne, you girls will be playing canasta mean as spit and eating lemon pound cake Ruthie made, and you'll be feeling just fine, Mom."

Even before we were married, Fritz called her "Mom." It had increased his standing in my eyes by about thirty percent.

The anesthesiologist came in and said, "She's ours, now!" He said it in a friendly way, but I didn't like it one bit.

We all kissed Mom, and she smiled wanly. "Bye, kids!"

Fritz and I went down to the cafeteria and had some breakfast. "You know, some people lose their appetite when they're worried," he told me.

I was drizzling a stack of pancakes with syrup. "They do?"

Later, when I came out of the restroom I caught Fritz at our table watching a baby in her high chair at the next table. The baby was sucking on a pancake, and her face was freckled with bits of it, and sparkling with syrup. The parents looked exhausted, but there was such unabashed yearning on Fritz's face, I had to look away. Fritz and I had been debating for months about whether it was time to start a family. He was sure; I wasn't.

After breakfast, Fritz had to leave to drive back to Austin.

Fritz kissed me good-bye in the elevator and held me till we reached the ground floor. "I wish I could stay, honey."

"I know you do." I didn't want to let go of him.

"She'll be fine, Roxpie," he promised me.

We kissed again, and I watched him go through the door to the parking lot. I went to a ladies' room and splashed cool water on my face to stave off tears, then rode back up to the surgery waiting room.

Dr. Redman found Joanie, Aunt Ruth, and me huddled around the TV eating powdered-sugar donuts. Dr. Redman had been our family doctor since forever; just seeing him made me feel better.

"Christina came through with flying colors," he told us. "She is A-okay. You can go see her at around three."

Joanie and I hugged, and Aunt Ruthie went over to talk to Dr. Redman.

"Yes," I heard him whisper to her. "It's a miracle she held onto them this long." He went back to the operating wing.

I sent Joanie downstairs for sandwiches and Cokes.

"Ruthie."

She glared at me slightly. She hated when I called her that, the suggestion that we were both adult women, including me. It didn't matter that I was thirty-two.

"Aunt Ruthie?"

"Yes, honey?"

"What did Doctor Redman mean that it was a miracle she'd held onto them this long?"

"Oh, you heard." Ruthie sat down and pulled at her stockings a little. She patted her hair. It had gone dead gray since I'd seen her last.

"Honey, I guess you never knew. Your mom almost died when Joanie was born."

"God." I sat down suddenly.

"Are you all right, honey?"

Ruthie grabbed my wrist and pinched it, her version of smelling salts. "They didn't want to scare you. They made me swear not to tell you, at the time. Gosh, honey, you were in high school. You had your clubs and your boyfriends and things. As soon as Christina was out of the woods, your dad said, this is our secret: there is no reason to worry Roxanne with this."

I had not been able to visit Mom for a couple of days after Joanie was born, I remembered that. At the time I didn't know that was unusual. I remember going to look at Joanie lying in her bassinet in the baby room. Usually she was shaking her little fist and wailing. Her hair was dark brown like Dad's, and it was so lush and dense that it nearly fell into her eyes. She wore a pink sleep sack and had a demeanor that suggested she was both cantankerous and sweet.

"What happened?" I asked Ruthie. "What went wrong?"

"The baby came out fine, but then Christina started hemorrhaging. No one knew why. When I got to the hospital your daddy was in the waiting room crying like a baby. They didn't know if Christina would make it. I'll never forget it. Frank couldn't handle seeing his brother like that; he paced up and down the halls while I sat in the waiting room with your daddy. He clean laid his head down on my lap and cried till my skirt was soaked. I kept reminding him that Joanie was okay, and he would say that was a blessing, but then he would take on some more about your mother and how he couldn't lose her. A man never loved a woman more than your dad loved your mom. But you know that."

I began to cry myself.

Joanie came off the elevator with bags of food from the cafeteria and a stack of Coke cups that teetered dangerously. She saw me crying and froze there.

Ruthie said, "Lord, she thinks Christina is in trouble."

I rushed over to Joanie. "Everything is fine," I told her. "I was tired and relieved and I just broke down."

"Jesus, Roxanne, I thought—"

"I know, I'm sorry."

We ate greasy grilled cheese sandwiches, potato chips, pickles, and Cokes. I wanted to ask Ruthie more, but now wasn't the time.

When we went in to see Mom, her skin was the bluish white of skim milk, and she looked flattened out. The IV worried me, but of course it was normal after surgery. She was still completely woozy from anesthetic.

"Hello," she said, very slowly. It seemed as if the word had taken a lot of effort.

Joanie sat beside her and began to tell her everything about the pizza party she'd been to the night before, like this was just a conversation at the dinner table any day. She talked on and on. "Uh huh," Mom would answer. Or "Uh huh?" Her eyes would shut and then swim open. She dozed off a couple of times, and Joanie just went on, talking about how hard it was to find a summer job and what to wear when she went out with Cliff next Saturday.

Cliff? Joanie had a boyfriend?

I sat on a chair across the room and held onto the arms firmly. I had never noticed before how much Joanie looked like Mom. Joanie's hair color was dark brown like Daddy's, but her face was almost identical to Mom's, with the delicate widow's peak and her thin, beautifully curved lips. Joanie wore jeans and a T-shirt, with a vest . . . Christ, Daddy's old Father's Day vest.

Joanie has an oddly accurate memory of Daddy, odd because Daddy died when she was four. She can remember everything important about him: how he clapped his hands when he figured out the crossword puzzle, or when his baseball team, the Texas Rangers, won, how he rode his own bike very slowly beside her while she rode her trike. She remembers him secretly taking her for double-scoop ice-cream cones, drenched in chocolate shot, too close to dinner. Mom inevitably found him out though, when they got home. Joanie's blackened teeth and the sprinkles all down her dress gave them away.

As recently as last Christmas Joanie came down to the tree Christmas morning wearing Daddy's old red-and-black flannel robe, which Mom has sewn back together again many times. We still hang Daddy's Christmas stocking every year. There is a tiny hole in the bottom where a candy cane went through once, but we wouldn't mend that.

I can remember explaining this to Fritz once when he remarked on how sad it was that Joanie missed growing up with my dad.

"But she didn't," I said.

I slipped out of the room later in the afternoon and tracked down Dr. Redman. "Is she really okay?" I asked. "Tell me the truth."

"She's doing great, Roxanne," Dr. Redman said. "Your mom's a trouper."

"Ruthie just told me about what happened to Mom when Joanie was born. I like to have died. I had no idea. Seems like I must have been the world's most oblivious fifteen-year-old."

"God, no, Roxanne. You were pure normal. Look at Joanie."

"You're probably right there. Did Mom really almost die?"

"I prepared your father for the worst. Well, I tried . . . he could hardly bear it. We were all scared that night: the nurses, a specialist I called in. Me, for sure. I had delivered a lot of babies, and had never seen hemorrhaging quite so bad."

"She's . . . but now. She's okay now? Was the surgery a hundred percent normal?"

"It was, Roxanne; she is really okay. She just had some fibroids that were causing her a little trouble, so we took them out. *It isn't cancer.* She's having a normal recovery."

"An excellent recovery?" The word excellent always reassured me.

Dr. Redman smiled and murmured, "Excellent."

★　　★　　★

115

Aunt Ruthie drove Joanie and me to their house for steak and potatoes. My Uncle Frank's great love in life, after Ruthie and Tommy, was his barbecue cooker. He greeted us at the door with a whiff of mesquite coming off him and a barbecue fork held high in a salute. "Christina's good?" he asked.

"She's good," Aunt Ruthie agreed. "Baby, bring me a very tall gin and tonic with a handful of limes, in a frosted glass!" she told Uncle Frank. She collapsed on the couch, kicked off her shoes, and rubbed her foot against her leg like a cat.

I was startled that they still called each other "Baby." It seemed oddly sexy, especially for Frank and Ruthie, but you never knew.

"Good heavens, you're looking beautiful!" Frank told me. He hugged me and said how great it was I could come be with Mom. "I *told* Ruthie we should call you," he whispered to me. "Roxanne, what will it be, a G & T?" he said, in a normal voice.

I realized how tired I was. After Uncle Frank handed me a drink I slipped off to lie down in the guest room. I sipped my drink and talked to Fritz on the phone. He told me he was about to sell his '52 Harley. "Man, I'll miss her," he said wistfully. All his vintage bikes were female. Sometimes I was jealous. He told me what he was eating for dinner: a big plate of sardines and Saltines. When I was away he relished meals of foods I despised.

Tears began to roll down my cheeks.

"What?" Fritz said. Even when I cried noiselessly, which I often did, he could tell.

"I found out today that Mom almost died having Joanie."

"Steak's on!" I heard Uncle Frank shout.

The next morning, Aunt Ruthie came to our house and made scrambled eggs for Joanie and me, as if we wouldn't know how to make our own breakfast. Scrambled eggs were rife with significance back in my house in Austin. First, they were the source of arguments early in our marriage. Fritz liked his eggs runny; I liked them dry. It took us a year to realize we could scoop a spoon out for him wet, then cook mine dry.

This last spring, a fight had ensued when Fritz complained about the aging carton of eggs in our refrigerator. He was indignant that I didn't check expiration dates regularly.

"You keep waffling on this baby thing, and *your* eggs will be too old to scramble," he yelled at me.

We glared at each other a terrible minute or two. The coffee carafe I was holding was suddenly too hot. Then we both started giggling at the same instant. "Waffles, eggs. Do you want a baby or a full-course breakfast?" I said.

After breakfast we made love. It was then that Fritz started the habit of sighing every time he heard my diaphragm case crack open. It was a discouraging thing having the act of love preceded by a resounding sigh.

117

When we went to the hospital Mom still looked pale. "I can't get that nurse to give me coffee for love or money." She looked on the brink of tears. When I kissed her forehead, her skin was cool and papery.

"Does it hurt much?" Joanie asked.

"Don't worry, honey," Mom answered.

I saw Mom flinch when Joanie plunked herself on the edge of the bed.

Ruthie entered the room. "Good news!" she exclaimed. "Dr. Redman says you can eat lunch."

Uncle Frank looked a little scared when he first came into the room. Had he ever seen my mother without lipstick? "Good heavens, you make it sound like food at the hospital is some kind of treat," Uncle Frank teased.

"It is when it's your first meal in thirty-six hours or so," Ruthie said.

Uncle Frank handed Mom a package. She opened it up, and it was a pale periwinkle bed jacket, with little accordion pleats at the wrists and neck. "A bed jacket," she said, with amazement. "They don't make these anymore!"

"I know," Frank said, grinning. "I ferreted away some stock

like that, from the good old days. This is something Carl ordered the spring before he passed, if you can believe it."

I helped Mom slip the bed jacket on over her gown. She moved very carefully and bit her lip in pain. She asked me for her lipstick, and when she put it on, with her bright pink lips and her hair banded back, she looked like a young girl.

Uncle Frank left to go to work. Ruthie suggested we play "Go Fish!" but Mom wasn't up to it. We turned on *Donahue*, but Mom was asleep by the time the first commercial came on. Her face looked still and serious, and her breathing sounded slightly labored. Joanie and Ruthie slipped out, and I stayed behind to smooth her pillows. Ruthie had to go grocery shopping, and Joanie disappeared after we all agreed to meet at Doreen's later.

I tracked down Dr. Redman, and told him Mom didn't seem right to me.

"That's just how people are after surgery, Roxanne," he said. "She'll be a bit better when you see her this afternoon, a lot better when you see her tomorrow. Some things can't be rushed."

"Dr. Redman, I can't stop thinking about how Mom almost died when Joanie was born."

"That was scary, I won't lie, but it was a freak thing. Which means, by the way, that there's no reason to worry you or Joanie would have any problems with childbirth. And this hysterectomy your mom just had, it was no different from most. No worse because of what happened back then."

Reassured, I walked downtown. I made a beeline for Doreen's Drugstore every time I was in Annette. I strolled up and down the aisles looking at hair barrettes, Frost and Tip kits, packs of Necco wafers, tins of shoe polish. I lingered at the baby products aisle. I held onto a blue rubber teething ring for a very long time, as if it were some sort of talisman, something that would answer my questions. I bought it and took the tag off and buried it deep in my purse to see what powers it might have over me.

Then I sat on the twirl seat at the marble counter and watched

Herbert split and fry me a frankfurter in real butter. He even toasted the bun on the grill. They still had the bosomy Coca-Cola glasses, filled to the rim with tiny squares of ice, splashed with Coke syrup and fuzzed with soda water. I thought of my summers with Denny Holer, when I was in high school. During the whole two years we'd dated, he'd worked here, after school and summers. I remembered his brown rippling muscles as he quartered lemons with quick swipes of his knife, or tapped the metal milk-shake flask against the recalcitrant milk-shake machine. I wondered what had become of Denny.

He stuck with me where many boys wouldn't have, even kept me company while I baby-sat for Joanie. I feared the odor of diapers would scare him off, but Denny smelled talcum powder, he said, Baby Magic, the sweet scents of baby care. We'd be flat on the couch making out till my lips were puffy, all my Maybelline lipstick eaten away. My hand would be on his crotch, his hands planted on my breasts, and Joanie would let out screaming upstairs. We would sigh and rearrange our clothes, and I'd go upstairs to get her while Denny put a fresh stack of 45's on the hi-fi.

"There's a kind of hush, all over the world . . . " drifted up the stairs. I'd change Joanie's diapers so fast I'd stick her or me or both of us with the diaper pins. Then I'd come downstairs and pour up some Similac for Joanie, some Cokes for Denny and me, and I'd sit her on the couch with her bottle propped up on a bunch of pillows. While Denny and I slow-danced in the dark we heard Joanie's loud slurping. I wonder sometimes what effect this may have had on Joanie, spending her infanthood in this lust-steeped teen world. Her screams and colic and spit-ups and runny poops were a powerful form of birth control for Denny and me during this time.

Though I loved Joanie, loved having a sister even if I couldn't confide in her yet, I had felt for many years that I did not want to have children. I have already done that, I would think. I had seen my mother mowed down by Joanie. I begrudged Joanie the teen parties her babyhood robbed me of. Now . . . now I didn't know what I thought.

I sat at Doreen's counter and closed my eyes and twirled. When I'd completed my circle I opened my eyes, and there Joanie stood, looking serious and stolid.

"Is Mom okay?" I whispered.

"Yeah, sure," Joanie said. She sat beside me and kicked her feet against the metal rung of her seat.

"I remember twirling you on that seat till I thought you'd take flight. You loved it," I said.

"Ha! Except the time I puked soft-serve vanilla on the floor!" Joanie seemed delighted with herself.

I said, "Joanie!" and heard my mother's voice coming out of me.

120

Joanie ordered a Coke with a double shot of syrup and a patty melt.

"Let's get a booth," I said.

We sat in the back. I could see "D. H. hearts R. M." over Joanie's shoulder. Denny Holer loves Roxanne Milner. "Have you lost your virginity?" I whispered.

"I'm scared to," Joanie answered.

"Good," I said.

She told me about her boyfriend, Cliff. Mom had never told me about him. Was he a complete mystery to her, too?

"Is he pressuring you?"

Herbert brought over Joanie's lunch. Joanie took a huge bite of sandwich and said, "Yo, hot," through a large wad of food. "Nah."

"Maybe he's scared, too," I said.

"Maybe. Don't worry, Mom told me all about birth control."

"*Mom* did? What a scream!"

"Yeah." Joanie laughed. "It was funny."

We ate dishes of chocolate chip ice cream. "Here comes Ruthie!" Joanie sing-songed. And Ruthie was upon us with stories of being snubbed by a shoe salesgirl at JCPenney. It was time to go back to the hospital.

So we could keep talking, Joanie and I sat together in the backseat. We waited while Ruthie adjusted all the mirrors, which she did each and every time she got in the car.

"Maybe you should stop," Joanie whispered.

"Stop what?" I answered.

"Birth control."

I was speechless.

"I want to be Aunt Joanie. I could come stay, help out with the baby during school vacations."

"You'd do that for me?"

"Sure. I know you baby-sat for me a billion times when I was a baby. I figure I kind of owe you."

"Girls, didn't your parents ever tell you it is *rude* to whisper?" Ruthie bellowed cheerfully.

My fingers slipped to the bottom of my purse and curled around the teething ring.

The second day Mom was home from the hospital, I was in the kitchen, making homemade tomato soup, her favorite. As I stirred the pot, a rich, sharp smell rose up to me, and I closed my eyes and inhaled. I loved this kitchen as much as I loved some people. This was the house I'd lived in from infanthood on up. When Joanie came they built on an addition, but otherwise it was much the same as when I was a little girl. The kitchen walls were pale lemon, repainted many times, but always that shade. There were the same white scalloped curtains with yellow cross-stitching and a wall pocket shaped like a flowerpot, which always held Mom's keys and used to hold Daddy's. I had licked, cumulatively, cupfuls of cake batter and icing off wooden spoons and mixer beaters here in this room. My mom used to joke that if I weren't careful my tongue would get stuck between the little metal bars of the beaters.

I laid out a big tray with a china bowl full of soup, a saucer of oyster crackers, and a linen napkin. I carried the tray into the living room. Mom was lying on the floor face-down by the couch. *Jesus Christ.* I froze for a second, till a hot splash of tomato soup hit my bare foot. I slammed the tray down on the coffee table and crouched beside her.

"Mom?" I asked, my voice quavery.

Mom swiveled her head around and said, "What, honey?" Her face was pinkened, but she looked alert.

There was a little dust bunny clinging to her hair at the temple.

"Mom, what happened? Did you fall down or pass out?"

"Heavens, no! I just dropped my pencil when I was doing the crossword puzzle. I wanted to grab it before I forgot this word: hospitable."

Sure enough, her hand swept out from under the couch holding a neon pink pencil.

"You scared me to death!" I told her.

"Well," my mother said. "If I had a nickel for every time I said that to you when you were growing up."

I helped her up and got her settled on the couch. My fingers trembled slightly as I removed the dust bunny from my mother's hair. "Homemade tomato soup for lunch," I told Mom.

"What's that on your foot?" Mom asked.

I spread an afghan on her legs. "Homemade tomato soup."

After lunch we ate an entire package of Lorna Doones and drank a whole pot of coffee. "Mom, Fritz wants us to get pregnant, and I can't decide."

"There's nothing I'd love more than a grandbaby, you know. I've been wondering, but I hate to push."

"Mom, I found out you nearly died when you had Joanie."

My mother put her fingers to her temples, her lifelong gesture of worry or exasperation. Her eyes got teary. "Honey, nowadays that wouldn't happen. There are all kinds of new medical things. That wouldn't happen to you."

"I know. But Mom, you almost died."

"But I didn't die. You know, nobody but your father ever knew this, but when things looked bad for me, I told Daddy that if I died he should get married again right away. I even told him who to marry."

"Mom!"

She was laughing softly to herself.

"Who?"

"Miss Fernstem. The librarian, do you remember her? She moved to Dallas when you were in high school. I thought she'd be a good mother, but she wasn't pretty. I would have always been known as Carl's beautiful first wife."

"Mom!" I pulled on her fingertips. I did that all the time when I was a child. Mom swore I'd made her fingers longer.

"You girls are the best thing that ever happened to Daddy and me. Even with Joanie a teenager, I can still say that, and that's saying a lot. She's worse than you were!"

"Don't you ever think Daddy's heart attack came from us being . . . too much?"

"Honey, did you think that?" Mom took my hand and pulled my fingers gently. "Of course not, Roxanne. Well, only if you made his heart too jumbo-sized for his chest. He was nuts for you girls."

"Nuts for you."

"Yes."

Fritz was exactly right in his prediction about Mom's recovery, as it turned out. He drove up on Sunday morning, bringing a bouquet of carnations to the door, and what did he see when he peeked through the screen door but Mom, Joanie, Aunt Ruthie, and me playing canasta. Ruthie had accused Mom of cheating, as she always did, and we were eating thin slices of Ruthie's lemon pound cake, tart and buttery slices with crispy sugar edges.

"Frank, put another pot of coffee on, Fritz is here!" Ruthie shouted.

*　　*　　*

Fritz and I left late that afternoon to drive back to Austin. Mom kissed my forehead like she used to when I was little, and Joanie, who was my height already, let me hug her. Aunt Ruthie's voice trailed us down the front steps; she was telling us where to eat on the highway. Uncle Frank was laughing. I could hear them faintly, even after we got into the car. I reached into my purse to take out my car keys, but instead I pulled out something blue and bumpy.

"What's that?" Fritz asked.

And I told him.

A Troll Named Beatrice Helps Out

"WHERE WERE YOU LAST NIGHT?" I ASKED TOMMY.
HE SAT AT MY KITCHEN TABLE HOLDING A BIG
yellow mug of black coffee. His hair was spiked with dirt, and his
T-shirt and jeans were torn and filthy. Still, my cousin looked
handsome.

I had an urge to strip him down as you do a child, and to
plunk him in the tub while I washed his clothes. He just stared at
me, like he couldn't figure out what I was doing there.

"Where—"

"Went to hear some music at Liberty Lunch. Reggae. I met
a girl and went home with her."

"Mmmm-hmm. Then why aren't you drinking her coffee this
morning?"

"She didn't have any?" Tommy grinned his slightly crooked
grin at me.

I sat down and was, as usual, putty in his one hand.

"Even with hair that dirty, you can have your pick, can't you?"

Tommy laughed. "Dirty hair, dirty clothes, and minus one
arm. Can you beat that? Got anything to eat?" Tommy looked
around, waiting for some food to materialize.

I went to the refrigerator and pulled out a can of biscuits. I
melted a half stick of butter and in another bowl I mixed cinnamon
and sugar. I whacked the can against the counter (for no good
reason, I loved whacking biscuit cans) and then separated the globs

of white dough. Twist into a winsome shape, butterize, and dredge in cinnamon sugar. "And that's how you make instant cinnamon buns!" I told Tommy, as I placed the tray into the oven.

I turned to see him sound asleep on my kitchen table. I walked over and petted his hair . . . or, I wanted to, but it was too gritty to truck with. When the oven bell rang, he sat up with a start and saluted. Vietnam was thirteen years ago, but in Tommy's sleep, the war was still in progress. "What the . . . Shit!" he noted. He was always embarrassed to be caught saluting, but anyone who'd seen Tommy wake up had seen this.

I set the plate of buns on the table and before I could blink an eye, Tommy had inhaled half a dozen. "Got any more coffee?" Tommy said, his mouth full of food.

126

I poured him coffee, and poured myself some milk. I tore the buns apart and ate them, little piece by little piece, but still I soon caught up with Tommy.

"Milk!" Tommy roared. "How come you're not drinking coffee?"

I pointed to my belly, which was half full of biscuits, half full of baby. I hadn't seen Tommy in months, and I was wearing a big terry-cloth robe; perhaps he thought I'd taken to packing a mixing bowl in my robe.

Tommy looked like he'd seen a little flying saucer resting on my belly. "Whoaa!"

"Ruthie told you I was pregnant."

"She did?"

"Well, surely . . ."

"I guess I've trained myself to hear only half of what Mom says. Huh, sometimes I miss the good parts. It's good, right?"

"Yep, Fritz and I were trying and everything."

"So, I'll be an uncle!"

"Not exactly. Second cousin or something? But he can call you Uncle Tommy, if you want."

"You bet. Can I take a shower?"

"Please!"

* * *

I put some of Fritz's old jeans and a T-shirt in the bathroom for Tommy, along with clean towels. Once Tommy was in the shower, I began to question him through the bathroom door. "Are you living on the street?"

I heard a lot of sloshing and spitting sounds. The baby did a little flip.

"Am I who?"

"Are you living on the street?"

"Maybe," Tommy bellowed.

"It seems like a yes or no question to me!" I bellowed back.

"Are you going to tell Mom?"

"No!"

"I'm living on the street."

I dragged a chair into the hallway and continued. "For how long?"

"How long I been there, or how long do I plan to stay there?"

"Take your pick, kiddo."

"I've been there a week. I'm off the street as soon as a sympathetic relative lets me move in. Anyone. Any sympathetic relative will do . . ." Tommy began whistling plaintively. It was "The Farmer and the Cowboy Should Be Friends," from *Oklahoma*. He began to sing, in an operatic voice, "One man likes to push a plow, another man likes to kick a cow. . . ."

He had a surprisingly beautiful voice. The surprise was how I'd forgotten.

Fritz snuck up behind me, back from his morning run. "Is that a man I hear singing in the shower?" he asked in a teasing, but slightly apprehensive way.

"Oh, yeah." I swatted his butt with a towel. "That reminds me, cinnamon buns in the oven!"

"And this man in the shower would be . . . ?"

"Let's see, if it's Tuesday, it must be . . . Tommy. My scoundrel cousin."

Fritz shouted, "Bonjour, Tommy!"

127

The sloshing sounds paused. "Fritz? Hey Fritz, way to go, on the baby!"

"Thank you. I tried my best," Fritz answered. "Man, did you leave me any hot water?"

"You got an extra toothbrush?" Tommy hollered.

While Tommy dried off and dressed, Fritz and I whispered in our bedroom. "Do you mind if Tommy stays here awhile?"

"Is 'awhile' two months, like last time?"

"No. God! No, we'll put a limit on it."

"Good luck!"

"Well, the baby is a good limit setter. He'll have to be out before the baby comes."

"Right, there's no room for two in our Sears Dream-o-Crib."

"And, he has to look for a job."

"Uh, double good luck."

As Aunt Ruthie liked to say, Tommy was smart as a whip and he cleaned up real well. But he had a lot of trouble sticking to things. He was nine hours short of a degree in botany. He had deejayed for the university radio station, but had never tried to get a "real job" at a station. He had dabbled in many things, but most ended after a few months. His last job was selling gourmet cookies for a store downtown, but he got in trouble for baking the cookies till they were done. These were the days when gourmet chocolate chip cookies were sold as "soft, melty, gooey," when, in fact, they were just plain underbaked.

Fritz dropped Tommy at the university employment office on his way to his job teaching music theory there at the college. Of course, you could drive a Tommy to water, but . . . But as always, Fritz had done all he could.

Sometimes when I couldn't find a good sleeping position at night, I slipped into the living room with a handful of marshmallow chocolate cookies and a glass of milk and sat on the couch watching whatever was on the old movie channel. The baby preferred Cary Grant movies, and so I began to think it might be a girl. I, too, was mesmerized by his dark and tender brow, the curvaceous chin. Recently I'd watched *Bringing Up Baby*; when Cary Grant put on Katharine Hepburn's slinky transparent pink wrap with the boa feather trim, I had laughed so hard I'd wet my pants, which isn't so hard to do when you're pregnant. Even though the movie was in black and white, I just knew the robe was pink. Not only did I wet my pants, but I kicked off a series of frantic hiccups from baby. The hiccuping was such a crazy sensation, as if my uterus and stomach were tangoing. For a moment I thought it was my water breaking, but no. My due date was still a few weeks away.

129

On Tommy's first night at our house, he was, of course, not at our house, but out. I was in front of the TV, watching Barbara Stanwyck toss her cornsilk hair at Fred MacMurray and eating Fritos with bean dip and salsa. Tommy came in at 3:30, and didn't seem surprised to find me up. He sat cross-legged on the floor by the coffee table and began scarfing chips and dip right along with me. I told him how Barbara Stanwyck had managed to dupe Fred MacMurray, and Tommy told me about a prospect he had working as a bouncer at a bar downtown.

"Think I can bounce with one arm?" he asked me. He playfully tapped my cat, Zippy, with the back of his hand. Zippy meowed; he was only hanging around hoping for a little taste of bean dip, which Tommy let him lick off his fingertips.

I can't remember how *Double Indemnity* ends exactly, because I fell asleep before then, but I do remember waking up to see Tommy across the room with his hand emerging from my purse, a fifty-dollar bill in tow. I shut my eyes again and tried to think what to do. If he needed the money that badly, should I ignore it? Mercifully, I fell back to sleep again and didn't have to deal with it. When I woke later I wondered if it was just one of my odd, hormonally altered dreams. But my wallet proved otherwise.

★   ★   ★

The next night I returned home at 12:30 A.M. I had been working the late shift at the university library, which stayed open till midnight. It had been hours since Fritz and I had met for dinner on campus, and I was starved. The baby was kicking and each kick felt like a little cry for ice cream. Standing at the refrigerator, I plunged a spoon into a pint of Blue Bell Dutch Chocolate. I had not even stopped to put down my purse or kick off my shoes. By the light of the refrigerator door, I saw Tommy doing push-ups in the dark living room. I heard him panting wildly. I walked in and asked him, "Ice cream?"

He plunked himself down on the wood floor and moaned a bit.

"How many?" I asked. I heaved myself into an armchair and shaved ice cream off the top of the carton and into my mouth.

"Many?" Tommy inquired.

When he looked up at me I could see his pupils were dilated to the size of dimes. Speed freak. I knew it in an instant. I'd had a speed-freak boyfriend once.

Now I knew why he was slim even though he could eat a dozen cinnamon buns in a heartbeat. "Where are you getting it?"

"Getting what?"

"The speed."

I could see a wash of fabrications and evasions flicker across those huge pupils, but when he opened his mouth the truth came out. "I know some guys in a band."

I shifted in my seat and the baby seemed to flip clean over. I sucked several spoonfuls of ice cream off my spoon, then planted the utensil in the ice cream and set it on the coffee table. "It doesn't seem to be doing you much good," I said softly.

Tommy laughed. "Nah," he admitted.

"What do you like about it?" I asked. I had tried it once during college while studying for finals, but didn't like it. It made me jittery and cranky.

"I started doing it in Nam. You have to keep awake if you're on night watch, or your butt is dead."

"You've been doing it since then?"

"Nah. After the morphine from my arm, it paled in comparison. I just drank myself silly for a while."

I remembered. "How long on the speed?"

"About a year. Staying awake beats the hell out of nightmares about Nam every night. Christ. It's been thirteen years."

"How about seeing someone?"

"Someone?"

"A counselor, a shrink, whatever."

"Do I look that bad?"

"Well, Tommy, you never look exactly bad, being as you're drop-dead handsome, but you've got an edge that isn't too pretty. And living on the street is not exactly a healthy lifestyle."

"Listen to you. You sound like a mom."

"Hey, don't say that like it's a bad word. But I am about to become one. I can't take care of you. You get some help, or you can get out of here."

I picked up my ice cream and began to eat again.

"Okay." Tommy looked at his feet.

"No, I mean it. I'm driving you there, and I'm sitting out in the waiting room while you're in there. You're not getting out of it."

"I don't have any money."

"The V.A. hospital, you can get help for free. And you need to apply for your benefits again anyway, to tide you over."

"Tide me over?"

"Well, you obviously need money. I saw you *borrowing* fifty from my wallet." My stomach knotted up and made the baby twitch.

"Roxanne, I'm sorry." Tommy hung his head, looking like he had when he'd been caught smoking in the garage when he was twelve.

"Don't be sorry, pay it back."

"I will." Tommy hugged me around my neck and snuck a bite of ice cream.

*   *   *

In the morning Tommy was gone. It took me a day or two to figure out he was really gone, given the kind of hours he kept. I cried, because who would eat all the blueberry muffins I'd baked? Fritz cleverly put some in the freezer for after the baby was born; people were warning him I'd have no time to cook when the baby came, and he'd started ferreting away leftovers all the time, like a kid stuffing crackers into his pocket at a restaurant.

A couple of weeks later Tommy's dad, my Uncle Frank, was hospitalized with chest pains. Aunt Ruthie called to tell me and to see if I knew where Tommy was. "We'll find him," I told Aunt Ruthie. "We'll be there as soon as we can. Kiss Uncle Frank for me."

"Oh, honey, they say it was just a little heart attack but how can a heart attack be little?"

I sent Fritz out into the night and he returned a few hours later with Tommy, collaring him like a cop bringing in a perp. Tommy looked wretched; he was shaky and drained of color.

"I found him. You don't want to know where," Fritz said.

"Put him in the shower," I told Fritz. "We'll clean him up and take him home."

"Is Dad going to be okay?" Tommy asked. His voice cracked, and as cranky as I was with him, it made me remember when he was thirteen and his voice was changing. I closed my eyes for a second to call up a picture of him then, his gold hair cotton-candy soft, his chin tipped with pimples, his eyes clear and transparent green. I opened my eyes, and it was hard to find that boy in there; his pupils took up the whole eye now, and there was only a smidgen of green shimmering at the edge. That was enough.

We readied ourselves for the trip to Annette. Fritz put enough pillows in the backseat of the car so that I could be surrounded. He was such a sweet expectant father I had pretty high hopes for his actual fathering. He also packed up the essentials: my home-made brownies and a thermos of milk. I couldn't have Fritos anymore; the doctor said I was retaining fluid, and the salt would not help matters. Fritz also insisted on loading up my going-to-hospital

bag, an odd collection that included two containers of baby powder but no diapers, a sunhat but no outfits. Well, I knew I wouldn't
need this stuff, but it made him feel better.

Tommy sat up front with Fritz, and I lay in back in my nest of
pillows while we headed up the highway to Annette. We were all
quiet for a while. It was the middle of the night, and the roads were
empty except for the occasional armadillo scuttling along the shoulder.

I fell asleep for a while, and when I woke the sun was coming
up; it was one of those miraculous early Texas summer morning
moments before the waves of heat simmer up and smack you in
the face. Tommy winked at me and passed me a little package. I
opened it up and inside there was a little troll doll, with fuchsia
hair flying in all directions. It was Beatrice, my troll from when I
was seven years old. Here it was more than a quarter of a century
later, and she looked pretty good, though a bit faded. And it
seemed her under-eye lines were deeper.

"Tommy!"

"I told you she'd turn up!"

When we were kids, Tommy had stolen my favorite troll. He
had told me he'd thrown it in Honey Lake, and all these years I'd
pictured her there at the bottom gazing up at the minnows. I had
never forgiven him.

"I can't believe you held onto her all these years."

Tommy laughed, and he sounded like his old self a little. "I've
just been saving her for your baby. That was my plan all along."

I reached up to bonk him on the shoulder and when I did,
splash. My water broke. For real this time, not some giggle-
induced pants-wetting. "Oh, shit."

"Hey, Rox, they say you should try to stop swearing before
the baby's even born," Fritz, oblivious in the front seat, said. "It
takes years to quit."

"I mean it, Fritz!" I started crying and laughing. "My water
broke!"

"Holy shit," Tommy hollered.

I saw Fritz's red curls bobbing wildly up front as he began to laugh. "I told you! I knew a car trip would bring it on!"

The hilarity halted when I had my first contraction, a searing pain that took my breath away. Fortunately, we were just driving into Annette. Good thing we were going to the hospital anyway.

I didn't exactly know it till they pried Beatrice out of my fist when they wheeled me into the delivery room, but I'd been clutching her in my hand since Tommy gave her back to me. I saw that Beatrice's wild pink hair was now compressed into a little snowball and my hand was pink. My mom and Aunt Ruthie were going wild running down the hallways of Annette Memorial Hospital. It was a dream come true for my mom that I would have the baby here in Annette, in the same hospital where I was born. I heard it picked up Uncle Frank's spirits to know his little grandnephniece, as he'd been calling the baby, was going to be born just two floors up from him.

Fifteen hours later, at 9:04 that evening, August 11, 1983, I was mom to a little girl. When she shimmied out of me the first thing I saw was her red hair, glistening mermaid hair the color of Fritz's. I knew then that her name was Sophie and told Fritz so. Sophies were sweet and spunky, I felt.

That night, Uncle Frank slept peacefully in the heart patient wing, though he told me later he dreamt Sophie was talking to him all night long "in a baby voice," he said. I slept hard, tired from labor, in the maternity wing. Fritz slept in a cot next to me, and baby Sophie Carla Beacon (the Carla was derived from my sweet departed daddy's name of Carl) slept some of the night in the nursery, some curled up to my breast. Tommy slept in the hospital, too; tomorrow he would be transferred to the V.A. hospital in Temple. His night was the hardest, no doubt.

In the morning I awakened to find my seventeen-year-old sister Joanie up at an hour unknown to her normally, all ready to put little dresses on Sophie.

"Honey, she's not a doll," my mother cried. "We don't want to bother at her."

Fritz held the baby while I got all checked out by Dr. Redman, who had delivered me and Joanie, and now Sophie. Fritz let Joanie put several colors of booties on Sophie, to keep her from trying to dress up my little one, who was just trying to sleep and nurse and didn't have a bit of fashion sense yet. We all agreed we liked Sophie in the apricot booties Ruthie had knitted best of all.

Fritz and I settled into Mom's house with Sophie for a week after we were released from the hospital. Mom had planned to come help us out in Austin, but since the baby had decided to be born in Annette, we thought we'd show our daughter her mom's hometown first thing. This thrilled Mom and Ruthie no end; they plowed through JCPenney, plucking pastel receiving blankets off the shelf like they were gathering rosebuds. Behind my back, Ruthie showed Fritz how to make formula; she knew full well I meant to nurse. And nurse I did. Mom's zip-up housecoats came in handy; one zip and Sophie had her breakfast at hand. I felt utterly at home with this baby at my breast. Fritz called her my "new necklace," as she was always nestled to my chest. But to me she was prettier than the loveliest jewels, with her garnet-colored hair that matched my engagement ring and matched, as well, her father's curls of red.

Joanie pitched in, though she looked close to passing out the first time she changed a messy diaper. As long as Sophie was clean and fragrant, Joanie was wild to hold her, and was already reading her the *Little Bear* books. I loved watching Sophie's stunned blinking on hearing about the time Little Bear made birthday soup. Sophie soon became the queen of the house, in her little pinstriped pink cotton jammies.

Fritz was an expert at walking her to sleep. He walked her around the block, holding her to his chest, till her little head fell over like an overripe rose petal. He whistled jazz tunes to her softly. This was something I had always known about Fritz, that he would be a wonderful father to our baby, as wonderful as my daddy had been to me.

The day before we left to go back to Austin, Tommy got a visitor's pass to come out of rehab to meet his newest little relative. His eyes were clearer and even his soul seemed calmed, or on the way there. What better remedy could there be for him than to hold my pink one in his arm? Uncle Frank was released from the hospital, too, and since he had to have bed rest, we brought Sophie to him and lay her on a pillow next to him. We watched them both nap for a bit.

Me, I was happy as could be for all the help and diversion, since it distracted me from the pain "down there," as Ruthie called it, and my sore nipples and my tiredness that was so deep I wanted to invent a new word for the feeling. But we were taken care of here in Annette's lap. Mom brought me ginger ale and compresses and often a freshly diapered Sophie for a feeding. My mother's smile when she held Sophie was a treasure I would take back to Austin with me, but still I ached on leaving. As we packed up the car with all our new baby accoutrements and, of course, one-week-and-a-half-old Sophie, I cried, wishing we could stay in Annette. Postpartum blues, I told Fritz. But no.

Cold and sweet

Had I ever missed a Fourth of July in Annette? The first time I brought Fritz to Annette, my hometown, he said she looked like an Annette all right; the pansies that grew in Annette Park were like flowers on a pretty girl's dress. Even the water towers looked like earbobs turned upside down. This was the home of the '62 Pie Fair after all, and almost three decades later there was still a mist of cinnamon powdering Town Square Gazebo like powder blush on a girl's cheek, still a perfume of vanilla in Honey Lake.

Fourth of July there was a parade of course, and though the temperature was ninety-eight, we were all there, with bells on, as Aunt Ruthie would say. Did say. My daughter, Sophie, would be six soon; she could barely contain herself. We let her run wild up and down the street, as all the downtown streets were cordoned off for the parade, and we knew she would be safe. She collected a balloon, a party popper, and a Tootsie Roll, on her route. Her sandals, pink strappy and new, glittered with the dust of Town Square.

We all stood and ate the iced fudge brownies that Aunt Ruthie had brought. Fritz's pale skin pinkened in the sun, threatening to match his riotous red hair. Sophie had come into this world with a coppery glint to her hair, but now it was a sort of dark strawberry-blond, and hung in a long sheet behind her, whispering to her tiny fanny.

My mother sat suddenly on the curb, and I did, too, to check on her. "You okay, Mom?"

"Heavens, yes. It's just so hot, and my feet hurt in these shoes."

I sent Fritz off to buy some iced teas at Doreen's Drugstore.

"Extra lemon!" my Aunt Ruthie trilled at his retreating figure.

Uncle Frank was in the hospital again; I was a bit surprised that Ruthie had come at all.

"I can't miss a parade; I'm like a kid," Aunt Ruthie said.

Uncle Frank was having heart pains once more, and had had his fourth heart attack. His attacks were small and easily remedied, it seemed; he'd never had a bypass or anything. Fritz said Frank's heart just needed a rest from Ruthie's tweakings, but that was mean.

Of course I had to wonder why it was that my uncle got to have only these small attacks, and my father, his brother, could just have the one. But whatever the reason, I was glad Uncle Frank was still in the world; I sure didn't begrudge him that, as much as I missed my father.

"Do you feel up to a trip to Dallas to shop for my wedding suit?" Mom asked. We were sitting in the shade now, in the gazebo, while the others still stood in the sun watching the parade.

"I wouldn't miss it!" I told Mom. My mom, a bride. I stroked her hair back and patted her forehead with a handkerchief I'd moistened at the water fountain. "That better?"

I worried about my mother, though in truth, she seemed to have a secret source of strength. She was only sixty-four years old, but then again, she was my only parent, too. So who could blame me for overreacting when she felt a bit faint in the sun?

"Mom, sometimes I think you waited all this time to get married again because you thought I couldn't handle it!"

Mom laughed softly. "Well, honey, could you have?"

I laughed, too. "Uh, no! Now I'm good, though. Hy's terrific." Hy was a gentleman farmer, my mother liked to say, but what this really meant was that he was retired and liked to garden. He grew tomatoes, big as saucers, and cantaloupe, the sweetest that ever passed my lips. Mom had known him since grade school. His first wife had died three years ago, and he had been going steady with my mom for two.

"Wait till you see the wedding band Hy got me. A pretty slip of gold with five tiny sapphires. I'm going to wear it up against your daddy's ring."

How could I not love Hy, a man who could comfortably nestle his ring up against Daddy's. He would be good to Mom.

Sophie sidled over to us and tugged on my shirttail. "Where's Daddy with the tea?"

As if she'd conjured him, Fritz appeared with a bouquet of paper cups in his hands, straws jostling each other.

Tommy's family would meet us later for a barbecue. I couldn't wait to see my cousin, whom I hadn't seen for two whole years. He and his wife Sally had been living in Oklahoma while she finished her degree in elementary education and feverishly tried to conceive. But they'd moved back to Annette and now had a new-born son named Jake.

Of all the funny ironies in life, here was the funniest to date. Tommy ran my dad's old lingerie store, Carl's Corsets. Incredibly, the name was the same as always, and the years had circled round to corsets being in again. Now, of course, they were called *bustier*, a word Tommy always had trouble pronouncing. "Burstier" was how he said it. Late in life, at forty, he'd discovered he had a head for business. And whom did he hire to manage the store day to day? My baby sister, Joanie. At twenty-three, she wasn't a baby anymore. She, too, was engaged, and she and Mom joked about a double wedding, but we seriously doubted this would come to pass. Joanie was marrying Mike Post, who had been her history teacher in high school. When she was his student, she had talked back to him every day and gotten the Civil War a trifle confused with some "other wars." He never let her forget this, of course.

I left Sophie with Fritz and Mom and Aunt Ruthie at the parade, and I made my pilgrimage to Doreen's Drugstore. Fritz often teased me that I was a junkie for that place. I couldn't wait to get a fix, the moment we drove into town.

I walked through the door and felt a fluff of A.C. immediately tickling my face. I made a beeline to the candy aisle and selected Tootsie Pops, Clark's clove gum, and Necco wafers. I popped over to the baby products aisle and picked out a jack-in-the-box for Tommy's son, Jake. Only Doreen's would have such an old-fashioned toy. Next, I went to the hair care aisle and bought some butterfly-shaped barrettes for Sophie's hair; I got bright blue ones to set off her red hair.

When I went to the front to pay, I nearly dropped my basket of items. There behind the counter was Denny Holer. But of course, it couldn't be. This boy was about fifteen, and Denny would be thirty-eight by now.

"You must be Denny's son. Jerry?" I said as I lay my treasure out on the counter before him.

"Yeah, Jerry. You know Dad?" he asked, as he rang up my purchases on the old-fashioned cash register.

"Yes, I went . . . we knew each other in high school. I knew your dad when he used to work here. He made a mean milk shake."

"Really?" When Jerry smiled, his lips curved up like Denny's had. He was a darling, surely popular with the girls at school.

"Oh, yes. I think I'm going to try one right now," I said. "I know it won't be as good as your dad's. Remember me to him, okay? My name's Roxanne Beacon, used to be Milner."

I sat down at a counter stool and laid my sack of purchases below the footrest. I beamed up at Herbert, whose hair had gone white all over, including his long mustache.

"Roxanne!" Herbert cried out. He bent to kiss my cheek and before I could say the words chocolate milk shake, he had the metal cup filled with vanilla ice cream. He lavishly squirted chocolate syrup onto the ice cream, added a splash of milk, then clamped the cup to the mixer.

"How's Doreen feeling?" I asked Herbert, raising my voice to be heard over the machine. I had heard from my mom that Doreen had been in the hospital recently.

"Honey, she's coming along real well. She'll be back here in a few weeks giving me heck about how I've run things while she was gone. You know Doreen." Herbert poured my milk shake into a tulip glass and handed me a straw and a spoon. "If you'll excuse me, sweetheart, I have to grill up some dogs for the kiddos." He gestured toward a family who sat in one of the booths behind me.

The cold chocolate nectar soothed my soul like nothing else. If only I could have one of these every single day, I thought. Austin had a few old-fashioned drugstores that served up milk shakes nearly as good as this one, but I had to fight city traffic to get to one. And after wrestling with the traffic, the milk shake could seldom quell my nerves.

I still loved Austin in many ways, but it had gotten a bit too big a city for me. Did I want Sophie to grow up in a town where young girls were held up by teenage gang members? Austin had fewer crimes than some cities, but on the other hand there was a rapist on the loose named after the highway he struck near. One not far from where we lived. All I could think of, as I noisily sucked on my straw to get the last bit of shake out of the glass, was how much I loved this place, how nothing in my life since Annette could match the way I felt here. I knew it was just a fantasy, but I wanted to come home for good, to live in Annette. I didn't talk about this much with Fritz, and certainly not with Sophie. I knew I was being neurotic and illogical; after all, small towns had drunks who could run over your children, date rapists, drugs, and all the rest of the woes of our world. In my head I knew that, but in my heart I most certainly did not.

After the Fourth of July fireworks, we all went back to Mom's place for a picnic. Since Uncle Frank was out of commission, Tommy and Fritz manned the barbecue, Hy made a pitcher of margaritas, and Mom, Joanie, Sally, and I made potato salad and three flavors of cobbler. Sophie tended baby Jake; she was a natural with little ones.

We stayed over for a few days after Fourth of July. Fritz wasn't teaching for the summer, and I was on an extended break from the library. Mom and I went shopping for her wedding suit. She and Hy would have an October wedding; by then there was a prayer the heat would have abated. We shopped in Dallas at Neiman Marcus. Mom found a pretty pink brocade suit and some fake pearls that were nearly as big as baby Jake's pop beads. Mom bought me a seersucker robe in rainbow stripes, then we had Reubens and Boston cream pie up in the restaurant.

Our last night in town we sat around the dinner table over at Aunt Ruthie's and Uncle Frank's. Frank was home from the hospital and couldn't sit up at the table yet, but we shouted conversation into the next room where he lay on the sofa wrapped up in a crisp white cotton sheet. Jake lay in a bassinet nearby looking remarkably similar to his grandpa in his white flannel baby blanket. Uncle Frank's remaining wisps of hair were soft and fine and fell to the center of his forehead, as Jake's hair did.

The whole family was there. I felt teary at the thought of leaving and going back to Austin the next day. I poured myself another cup of coffee and let a piece of Ruthie's homemade fudge melt in my mouth, my tongue toying with the walnut bits.

Fritz turned to me and took my hand in his. He had such an intense look on his face I got frightened. Whatever was it? Fritz turned my ring clear around my finger till the garnet swiveled face up again.

"What?" I asked Fritz.

"Let's go out back to drink our coffee. I've got something I want to talk about with you."

There were a few raised eyebrows around the table.

"Whuh-oh," Tommy teased, sounding like he was fourteen again.

I picked up my coffee and we went outside. I began to think

panicky thoughts. *Fritz is bored with our marriage. He forgot to pay the mortgage. He's got cancer.* "Honey, what is it?" I sat down suddenly on the glider swing, sloshing coffee all down my wrist. "Are you okay?"

"Honey, I'm fine. Relax! It's something good. What would you think if I got a job here in Annette? I hear they're looking for a new head of music at Richfield College."

Now I sloshed coffee down my bare knees. Boy. Good thing it had cooled off. "Are you serious? You'd like to move here?"

"If you'd like to. You think I don't notice your secret crying whenever we drive back to Austin?"

I laughed. A secret crier I was not. I always ended up choking on my sobs, but then I always made up some phony excuse for them, too: PMS, allergies, a Greta Garbo movie I'd seen on TV the night before. "God, honey. I'd love to move back here. But you've never lived in a small town. Would it make you nuts?"

"Naah. We spend so much time here, I think I know what the appeal is. It's pretty, um . . . soothing here. I'm so sick of traffic in Austin. And I worry about Sophie getting in trouble, when she gets older."

"You're a mind reader!" I clutched Fritz's hand.

"Well, I don't want to jump the gun; who knows if I can get on at Richfield?"

"They'd be crazy not to snatch you up."

"We'll see," Fritz said.

We held hands on the glider swing, swinging gently, till it grew dark around us.

A month later we were back in Annette to share our good news with the family. Fritz was to start his new job at Richfield September 1. I was beyond ecstatic. We had already talked to some realtors in Annette about renting a place till we had time to look for a house to buy.

All of us were gathered once more at my mother's dining table. As always, we were stuffed to the gills on a massive feast cooked by Mom and Aunt Ruthie. A fluffy light angel food cake ended the meal, though, a heartwise treat for Uncle Frank, who was still recovering from his heart attack. He was lying in the next room, overwhelmed by dinner. He always napped after a meal.

"Mom, I've got good news!" I blurted out. My voice squeaked like I was a girl.

Our real little girl, Sophie, took over for me. "Grandma, we're moving to Annette!"

"Oh my heavens!" my mom said. She came over and kissed me, then Sophie and Fritz. "Oh, honey!"

"Hot dog!" Aunt Ruthie shouted. "Frank, baby, wake up!" she hollered into the next room. "Roxie and Fritz and Sophie are moving home!"

"Hot dog!" Uncle Frank agreed.

"I'm going to head up the music department over at Richfield," Fritz said.

"All right!" Joanie exclaimed. "I can come take a class from you to help finish up my degree. Easy A, right?"

"Don't count on it, Joanie," Fritz answered. He gently punched her in the arm.

Tommy burst into laughter and lifted Sophie out of her chair. Over the years Tommy's one arm had become marbled with rippling muscles and seemed to hold the strength of several men. He could change his baby's diaper one-handed. Now, he lifted Sophie into the air and then onto his lap. Tommy's wife Sally kissed Sophie and said, "Ah ha! A future baby-sitter. Tommy, free baby-sitting!"

"Not free!" Sophie protested.

Joanie giggled. "Hey, kiddo, you can come help your old Aunt Joanie at the store sometimes. I'll teach you how to dress mannequins in nighties. Animal prints will be big this year."

Hy roared. "There's not going to be anything too scary in your trousseau, Christina, is there? An old man like me can't take animal prints; it would give my heart a scare."

"That's not what did it!" Uncle Frank shouted from the living room.

Aunt Ruthie turned a flashy burgundy. "Heavens," she said.

Fritz and I left Sophie with the family so we could go look at a few rental houses. We saw one with a creamy yellow kitchen like Mom's, and I knew we'd found our home. There was even a lease-to-buy option on the place. The other good news? It was *way* across town from Mom's house, and Aunt Ruthie's and Uncle Frank's. I wanted to be close to my folks, but I hadn't lost my mind! Also, the house was close to the public library. I hoped I might be able to get a job there eventually. And in the meantime, I might work as a volunteer, helping Mrs. Frenetti shelve books. That was the best way to find the juicy new titles.

Our first day in Annette my mom brought over a dish of hamburger casserole and a fluffy coconut cake and a case of Coca-Cola to "hold us" for a while. She also gave me, as a housewarming present, the wooden file cabinet that used to be in Daddy's study. Hy wanted to help carry it from the truckbed into our house, but Mom and I both protested. Luckily we still had a dolly around from the movers, so Hy's feelings weren't hurt. Fritz loaded it onto the dolly, then Hy got to push it up to the house. When I opened the bottom drawer I could smell just the teeniest scent of licorice; my father had always kept a stash in that drawer. Mom also brought over a vase of pansies and a basketful of tomatoes from her yard.

Ruthie ran by with pigs in a blanket and brownies and a huge watermelon. She hugged and kissed us all and then ran back to be with Uncle Frank, who was still needing some TLC from his last hospital visit.

I ran off downtown that afternoon on the pretext of needing to pick up some things like Spic and Span and some clothespins and paper towels. But, really, I just wanted to be downtown. I stopped off first at Carl's Corsets. There was a beautiful display in the window of a mannequin in a bridal negligee. The garment was pale pink silk with flowers of lace at the cleavage and a fallaway hem. The satin mules she wore were vanilla-colored. Honeymoon lingerie was the least changed fashion staple of all time. The only difference I could see, now that Tommy was in charge of the store, was that the mannequin looked a tad more busty than those of the old days, and the mules on her overarched toes were spike-heeled. When I walked into the store and saw Tommy behind the counter, I burst into giggles. He was wearing falsies on his head, like they were Mickey Mouse ears. Boy, did that bring back memories.

"Minnie?" Tommy hollered in a squeaky voice.

"That's me," I hollered back. "Do you wear those ears all the time?" I asked.

"No," he answered. "I was entertaining the Big Jake." Behind the counter, Tommy's son lay in his bassinet. I kissed the baby's feet and then looked into his intense green eyes.

"You will break a lot of hearts at Annette High," I told Jake. "Like your pop, here."

I leaned up and gave my cousin a kiss on the cheek.

Just then Joanie came out from the back of the store and hugged me. "I got you pink cotton panties!" she announced. She knew my taste in lingerie.

"Guess I'll be ordering these in regularly, now that you're back in town," Joanie said.

"Thank you very much," I told her. "Let me see your ring!" I examined Joanie's engagement ring, a pear-shaped sapphire. We girls had a tradition of stones other than diamond, for some reason.

"You girls always have to be different," Tommy teased.

"Nah," Joanie said. "We just *are* different."

"I'm off to Doreen's," I told Tommy and Joanie a half hour later, after I purchased the cotton panties and kissed Jake once again.

"Doreen-aholic!" Tommy teased.

I had to have some, and I had to have it right away. Doreen's niece Bertie placed the coffee saucer in front of me. It nearly overflowed with smooth, shivery frozen salad. I took my fork and speared a maraschino cherry. In my mouth it was a freezy cold sphere of heaven.

"Say," Bertie said. "You're Carl Milner's first baby girl, aren't you?"

"You bet I am." I smiled and licked whipped cream from the corner of my lip. I was home.

Epilogue

"WELL, I DIDN'T LIKE TO BAKE PIES WHEN I WAS YOUR AGE EITHER. NOT TILL ABOUT A WEEK BEFORE THE pie fair."

"Pie fair?" Sophie screeched. "Jeez, what was that? A fair is for riding roller coasters and stuff, not for pies."

Sophie twirled her long hair into a rope and twined it up to her neck and pinned it without even watching. When I was twelve I couldn't insert a bobby pin without looking in the mirror. Sophie was a vision; her hair was mermaid-wavy red hair, and she had more freckles than her daddy. What a beauty we had made!

"Okay, now that you've got your hair out of the flour, let's go." I pulled out my cherry pie recipe.

"Why is there that note about ice cream, Mom? Most recipes don't have little notes like that."

"Maybe they should," I told Sophie. I showed Sophie how to roll a crust gently, how to handle it like it was precious material. It was. I showed Sophie how to tell when the cornstarch has done its job, turning the pie juice from creamy pink to bright-jewel red. "Yep, dunk that butter in now!" I cried out.

When the pie was browned to a perfect color and smelled like heaven, we pulled it out of the oven and let it cool till we couldn't stand it. I cut us each a slice and we sat down at the kitchen table. When Sophie scooped the vanilla ice cream onto the pie it stayed cool and steaming on the top and melted into creamy pools around the pie.

"Okay, let me tell you about the pie fair," I told Sophie. "The summer of 1962, the year of the pie fair, I was wild for base-ball . . ."

Recipes

MARY WILLIS'S SWEET POTATO PIE

One 9-inch pie shell
2 cups cooked, peeled
  sweet potato, mashed till
  smooth
1½ cups evaporated milk
  or half-and-half
¼ cup brown sugar

½ cup white sugar
½ teaspoon salt
1 teaspoon cinnamon
½ teaspoon ginger
¼ teaspoon allspice
⅛ teaspoon cloves
2 slightly beaten eggs

Blend all ingredients together and pour into pie shell. Bake 15 minutes at 425°, then lower heat to 350° and bake 45 minutes longer or until an inserted knife comes out clean. Cool to room temperature.

Serve with sweetened whipped cream.

CHRISTINA'S LEMON MERINGUE PIE

1 baked 9-inch pie shell
1½ cups sugar
7 tablespoons cornstarch
dash salt
1½ cups water
3 beaten egg yolks
1 teaspoon grated lemon
  peel

2 tablespoons butter
½ cup lemon juice

Meringue:
3 egg whites
1 teaspoon lemon juice
6 tablespoons sugar

In saucepan, combine sugar, cornstarch, and salt. Stir in water. Bring to boil over medium heat and cook, stirring constantly, till thick, about 5 minutes. Remove from heat, stir small amount of hot mixture into egg yolks, then return to remaining mixture in pan. Bring to a boil and cook 1 minute, stirring constantly. Remove from heat. Add lemon peel and butter. Slowly stir in lemon juice. Cool to lukewarm. Pour into cooled baked pie shell. With electric beater, beat egg whites with 1 teaspoon lemon juice until soft peaks form. Gradually add 6 tablespoons sugar, beating until stiff. Spread meringue over filling, sealing to edges of pastry to avoid shrinking. Bake in preheated 350° oven 12 to 14 minutes or until meringue is brown. Cool thoroughly on countertop, then refrigerate till very cold. Serve cold! (Delicious with strong black coffee.)

DOREEN'S FROZEN FRUIT SALAD

3-ounce package softened
cream cheese (okay to use
light cream cheese but
don't use non-fat)
⅓ cup mayonnaise (okay
to use light mayo, but
don't use non-fat)
1 teaspoon lemon juice
⅓ cup sugar
1 cup whipping cream

⅔ cup miniature
marshmallows
¼ cup drained mandarin
orange slices
1 pound can fruit cocktail
(the kind with
maraschino cherries in
it), drained
2 tablespoons chopped
pecans

Blend cheese, mayo, lemon juice. With electric mixer, beat whipping cream, adding in sugar, a tablespoon at a time, until stiff. Fold this mixture into cheese mixture. Fold in rest of ingredients. Pour into 8-inch-square pan and cover with plastic wrap, then aluminum foil to seal. Freeze. Before serving, thaw slightly, cut into squares, and serve. Makes a nice side salad with sliced baked ham. Or a summer lunch for certain dads.

Serves 6 to 8.

CHRISTINA'S DUTCH CRUMB CAKE (CALLED SPICE CAKE IN STORY)

1½ cups sifted flour
1 cup sugar
¼ teaspoon cloves
¼ teaspoon allspice

½ cup butter
½ teaspoon baking soda
½ cup sour milk

Mix together flour, sugar, and spices. Cut in butter with pastry blender till crumbly. Reserve ½ cup for topping. Dissolve baking soda in sour milk and add to mixture, stirring just to blend. Grease an 8-inch-square cake pan. Pour in mixture and sprinkle with reserved crumb topping. Bake at 350° for 35 minutes or till brown and top is crispy looking. Serve warm.

Good with coffee. Good for breakfast or for afternoon treat. Good for making up with Daddy.

Mabel's Angel Food Cake
with Chocolate Sauce

1 cup cake flour, sifted
1½ cups sugar, divided
1½ cups egg whites (about
  10 egg whites)
2½ tablespoons water

1½ teaspoons cream of
  tartar
¼ teaspoon vanilla
1 teaspoon almond extract
½ teaspoon salt

Preheat oven to 350°. Resift the cake flour with ½ cup of the sugar. Sift together 5 more times. Combine the egg whites, cold water, cream of tartar, vanilla, almond extract, and salt. Beat with electric mixer till nearly stiff. Sift the remaining 1 cup of sugar. Fold it into the egg-white mixture about 2 tablespoons at a time, till all is folded in. Then gradually fold in the flour and sugar mixture gently. Pour the batter into an ungreased 9½-inch or 10-inch tube pan with removable insert. Bake about 45 minutes. When the cake is done, cool upside down 1½ hours, then remove from pan. Cut the cake gently with a cake divider into slices.

Pour warm chocolate sauce over a slice of cake.

Chocolate Sauce:

2 squares unsweetened
  chocolate
2 tablespoons butter

⅔ cup sugar
½ cup evaporated milk
1 teaspoon vanilla

Melt chocolate and butter. Add the sugar and evaporated milk. Cook until thick over low heat. Add vanilla.

AUNT RUTHIE'S HOT FUDGE SAUCE

1 stick butter or margarine
2 squares unsweetened
* baking chocolate*
1½ cups sugar

6 tablespoons milk
2 tablespoons Karo white
* corn syrup*

Melt the butter and chocolate over low heat. Add the sugar, milk, and Karo. Stir together and bring to a boil—boil for one minute. Take off heat and let set for about 2 minutes. Then pour while still hot over vanilla ice cream. It should harden a bit (not really hard, more chewy) when it hits the cold ice cream. Warning: highly addictive.

CHRISTINA'S BISCUITS

2 cups sifted flour   ½ teaspoon salt
4 teaspoons baking powder   ½ cup Crisco
2 teaspoons sugar   ⅔ cup milk
¼ teaspoon cream of
  tartar

Sift dry ingredients together. Cut in the Crisco with a
pastry blender. Mix in the milk, being careful not to overmix.
Knead gently in a few strokes and either pat or roll out to
about half-inch thickness. With a floured biscuit cutter, cut
the biscuits and place on ungreased baking sheet. Bake in preheated 450° oven for about 10 minutes or till browned.

Delicious hot, split, with butter and honey.

CHRISTINA'S LEMON SOUFFLÉ (ROXANNE CALLS THIS LEMON PUDDING CAKE)

1 cup sugar
2 tablespoons flour
1 tablespoon butter
Juice and grated rind of
  1 lemon

1 cup milk
2 beaten egg yolks
2 egg whites

Mix together sugar, flour, and butter to make crumbly mixture. Add juice and rind of 1 lemon. Add milk and beaten egg yolks. With electric mixer, whip egg whites and fold in. Put in casserole or soufflé dish and place in pan of hot water. Bake at 350° for 45 minutes. Cool on counter, then chill in fridge. Serve cold.

Scoop into serving dishes. A light, tart-sweet dessert, good after a heavy meal (for those who will forge ahead).

CHRISTINA'S BLUEBERRY MUFFINS

¼ cup butter
½ cup sugar
1 egg
¾ cup milk
¼ teaspoon vanilla
1¾ cups + 1 tablespoon
 flour

2½ teaspoons baking
 powder
½ teaspoon salt
1 cup blueberries, cleaned
 and patted dry

Cream butter and sugar. Beat in egg, then milk and vanilla, beat till nearly smooth. This mixture will seem very liquidy to you. Combine the 1¾ cups flour with baking powder and salt in small bowl. Add to milk mixture; stir just till dry ingredients are moistened (batter will be lumpy). Toss berries with remaining 1 tablespoon flour, then fold into batter. Spoon into 12 greased muffin cups. Bake in preheated 425° oven for about 25 minutes or till nicely browned. Turn out of tins. Serve hot!

AUNT RUTHIE'S
CINNAMON ROLLS

1 package dry yeast
¼ cup warm water
1 cup milk, scalded
¼ cup butter

¼ cup sugar
1 teaspoon salt
1 well-beaten egg
3½ cups all-purpose flour

Cinnamon Filling:

½ cup butter
1 cup sugar

1 tablespoon ground
cinnamon

Melt butter and stir in sugar and cinnamon.

Soften yeast in lukewarm water. Combine milk, butter, sugar, and salt (if the scalded milk isn't hot enough to melt the butter, put on very low heat till the butter melts). Cool to lukewarm. Add yeast and egg. Add flour in gradually, starting with about half the flour, then adding in the rest gradually. Stir vigorously. Let rise until double.

Divide dough into 2 parts. (This dough is a pleasure. It is soft and warm and tender, like a baby's bottom.) Roll first half of dough into rectangle 16 × 18 inches with floured rolling pin on floured surface. (Cover the remaining half with a towel while you work with the first half.) Put half of the cinnamon mixture on rectangle, spread to edges with knife or spoon.

Roll up jelly roll–style and then cut into 16 slices. Place in ungreased round cake pans (square pans can be used, but round creates better shapes). Repeat with other dough portion.

Bake rolls in preheated 375° oven for about 20 minutes or till lightly browned. Turn out of pan immediately (or they will stick like crazy) onto a serving plate and glaze with thin confectioners' sugar icing.

Makes about 32 small rolls.

AUNT RUTHIE'S LEMON POUND CAKE

2 cups all-purpose flour
½ teaspoon baking powder
½ teaspoon salt
*1 cup (2 sticks) unsalted
butter, softened*

1 cup granulated sugar
*5 large eggs, at room
temperature*
1 teaspoon vanilla
2 teaspoons lemon extract

Preheat oven to 325°. In a medium bowl stir together the flour, baking powder, and salt.

In a large bowl beat the butter with an electric mixer till fluffy. Gradually beat in the sugar till blended. One at a time, beat in the eggs, and then add the vanilla and lemon extract. Add the dry ingredients; beat just till smooth. Turn into a greased and floured 9 × 5 × 3-inch loaf pan, and bake till the top peaks and turns golden brown, about 1 hour and 15 minutes, till toothpick comes clean. Cool in pan on rack for 10 minutes, then turn out and cool thoroughly on rack.

The Sunday newspaper, a pot of coffee, and a slice or three of pound cake. But yes!

ROXANNE'S BROWNIES

1 stick butter
2 squares (one ounce each)
  unsweetened baking
  chocolate
1 cup granulated sugar
2 eggs

½ teaspoon vanilla
½ cup all-purpose flour
1 pinch salt
¼ cup chopped pecans
  (optional)

Melt butter and baking chocolate in saucepan. Remove from heat and stir in sugar. Add eggs one at a time, stirring well. Stir in vanilla. Stir in pinch of salt and flour. Stir in nuts, if using. Pour into lightly greased 8 × 8-inch pan and bake in preheated 350° oven for about 25 minutes or till knife inserted comes out clean. Cool till you can't stand it anymore (just a couple of minutes!) and then slice into squares and eat. Good alone, or with vanilla ice cream. People will fight over the chance to lick this pan. Rightly so.

MISS CHERRY PIE

1 recipe 9-inch double-
  crust piecrust
2 No. 2 cans sour red
  pitted cherries
2½ tablespoons cornstarch

1 scant cup sugar
2 teaspoons lemon juice
½ stick butter
¼ teaspoon almond
  extract

Drain one of the cans of cherries and discard the juice. Drain the other can's juice into a saucepan. Reserve the 2 cans of drained cherries in drainer. To cherry juice in saucepan, add cornstarch and sugar. Stir together, then heat to boiling. Boil gently till mixture is thick and clear. Put reserved cherries back into saucepan. Add lemon juice, butter, and almond extract, and leave over very low heat only till butter melts. Then remove from heat completely. Roll out one crust and line pie pan with crust. Pour in the cherries. Put the top crust on (be sure to cut steam slits). Bake in preheated oven at 425° for 10 minutes, then lower oven to 350° and cook another 30 minutes or till crust is lightly browned. Cool a bit before cutting. This pie cries out to be served with a scoop of vanilla ice cream on top, which is why the pie should be served warm!